国家出版基金项目
NATIONAL PUBLICATION FOUNDATION

"十三五"国家重点图书

中国南方民间文学典籍英译丛书

丛书主编 张立玉 丛书副主编 起国庆

E'BING

AND

SANGLUO

出品单位：

中南民族大学南方少数民族文库翻译研究基地

云南省少数民族古籍整理出版规划办公室

WUHAN UNIVERSITY PRESS

武汉大学出版社

娥并与桑洛

云南省民族民间文学德宏调查队 搜集整理

刘纯 英译 [美] H. W. Lan 审校

·汉英对照·

图书在版编目(CIP)数据

娥并与桑洛:汉英对照/云南省民族民间文学德宏调查队搜集整理;
刘纯英译.—武汉:武汉大学出版社,2020.7(2022.1重印)
　　中国南方民间文学典籍英译丛书/张立玉主编
　　"十三五"国家重点图书　2020年度国家出版基金资助项目
　　ISBN 978-7-307-21455-2

　　Ⅰ.娥…　Ⅱ.①云…　②刘…　Ⅲ.傣族—叙事诗—中国—汉、英
Ⅳ.I222.7

中国版本图书馆 CIP 数据核字(2020)第 060718 号

责任编辑:郭　静　　　责任校对:汪欣怡　　　版式设计:韩闻锦

出版发行:**武汉大学出版社**　(430072　武昌　珞珈山)
　　　　　(电子邮箱:cbs22@ whu.edu.cn　网址:www.wdp.whu.edu.cn)
印刷:湖北恒泰印务有限公司
开本:720×1000　1/16　　印张:12.5　　字数:149 千字
版次:2020 年 7 月第 1 版　　2022 年 1 月第 2 次印刷
ISBN 978-7-307-21455-2　　　定价:36.00 元

丛书编委会

学术顾问

王宏印　李正栓

主编

张立玉

副主编

起国庆

编委会成员（按姓氏笔画排列）

邓之宇　王向松　艾　芳　石定乐　龙江莉　刘　纯
陈兰芳　汤　茜　李克忠　杨　柳　杨筱奕　张立玉
张扬扬　张　瑛　和六花　依旺的　保俊萍　起国庆
陶开祥　鲁　钒　蔡　蔚　臧军娜

序

　　近年来，民族典籍英译捷报频传，硕果累累。韩家全教授等人的壮族系列经典翻译陆续出版，王宏印教授等人的系列民族典籍英译研究著作已经问世，李正栓教授等人的藏族格言诗英译著作不断在国内外出版，王维波教授等人的东北民族典籍英译著作纷纷付梓，李昌银教授等人的"云南少数民族经典作品英译文库"于 2018 年年底出版，其他民族典籍英译作品也在接踵而至。

　　近日，中南民族大学张立玉教授传来佳音：他们要出版"十三五"国家重点图书——"中国南方民间文学典籍英译丛书"。虽叫民间文学，其实基本上都是民族典籍。这一系列包括十本书，它们是《黑暗传》《哭嫁歌》《哈尼阿培聪坡坡》《彝族民间故事》《南方民间创世神话选集》《查姆》《召树屯》《娥并与桑洛》《金笛》《梅葛》。其中，好几本是云南少数民族的。只有一本是汉族典籍，即《黑暗传》。很有意思的是，这些典籍展示了不同民族的创世史诗或诸如此类的东西。

　　《黑暗传》以民间歌谣唱本形象地描述了盘古开天辟地结束混沌黑暗，人类起源及社会发展的历程，融合了混沌、盘古、女娲、伏羲、炎帝神农氏、黄帝轩辕氏等众多英雄人物在洪荒时代艰难创世的一系列神话传说。它被称为汉族首部创世史诗。《哈尼阿培聪坡坡》是一部完整地记载哈尼族历史沿革的长篇史诗，堪称哈尼族的"史记"，长 5000 余行，以现实主义手法记叙了哈尼族祖先在各个历史时期的迁徙情

1

况，并对其迁徙各地的原因、路线、途程，各个迁居地的社会生活、生产、风习、宗教，以及与毗邻民族的关系等，均作了详细而生动的辑录，因而该作品不仅具有文学价值，而且具有重大的历史学、社会学及宗教学价值。《南方民间创世神话选集》包括一些创世神话，主要是关于世界起源和人类起源的神话。本书所列包括生活在广泛地域的民族，如门巴族、珞巴族、怒族、基诺族、普米族、拉祜族、傈僳族、毛南族、德昂族、景颇族、阿昌族、布朗族、佤族、独龙族、水族、仡佬族、布依族、仫佬族、高山族和侗族等。这些神话不仅讲述了世界的起源，也讲述了人类的始祖，以及人类对世界的改造。《梅葛》是彝族的一部长篇史诗，流传在云南省楚雄州的姚安、大姚等彝族地区。"梅葛"本为一种彝族歌调的名称，由于人们采用这种调子来唱彝族的创世史，因而创世史诗被称为"梅葛"。《查姆》是一部彝族史诗，是彝族人民唱天地、日月、人类、种子、风雨、树木等起源的长篇史诗，被彝族人民当作本民族的历史来看待。

其余几本书展示了一些少数民族的风俗习惯、恋爱故事、斗争故事等。《哭嫁歌》是土家族文化典籍。"哭嫁"是土家族姑娘在出嫁时进行的一种用歌声来诉说自己在封建买办婚姻制度下不幸命运的活动，是指土家族姑娘的抒情歌谣，富有诗韵和乐感，融哀、怨、喜和乐为一体，以婉转的曲调向世人展示土家人独特的"哭"文化。《彝族民间故事》是一部以流传于云南楚雄彝族自治州彝族人民中间的民间故事为主体，同时覆盖全省包括小凉山等彝族地区的民间故事集。这些故事丰富多彩，从中能看到民族民间故事的各种形态和生动、奇妙而颇具彝族民族特色的文化特征。《召树屯》是傣族民间长篇叙事诗，叙述了傣族佛教世俗典籍《贝叶经·召树屯》中一个古老的传说故事。这部叙事诗一直为傣族人民所传唱，历久不衰。《娥并与桑洛》是一部优美生动的叙事诗，一个凄美的爱情悲剧。《金笛》是一部苗族长篇叙事诗，富于变幻性和传奇性，尽情铺叙扎董丕冉与蒙诗彩奏的悲欢离合，热情赞颂他们在与魔虎的激烈斗争中所表现出来的坚贞不屈、英勇顽强的精神，许多情节含有浓郁的民族特色。

这些故事都很引人入胜，都很符合国家文化发展需求，向世人讲述中国故事，传播中华文化，并且讲述的是民族故事，充分体现了党和国家对各民族的关怀。

民族典籍英译是传播中国文化、文学和文明的重要途径，是中华文化"走出去"的重要组成部分，是国家战略，是提高文化"软实力"的重要方式，在文化交流和文明建设中起着不可或缺的作用，对提升中国国际话语权和构建中国对外话语体系以及对建设世界文学都有积极意义。

中国民族典籍使世界文化更加丰富多彩、绚丽多姿。我国各民族典籍中折射出的文化多样性极大地丰富了世界多元、特色鲜明的文化。人们对多样性形成全新的认识角度和思维方式，有助于开阔视野，丰富思考问题的角度，挖掘这些经典中的教育价值和文化价值，对世界其他民族都有指导和借鉴意义，并且有助于建设我国的文化自信。

民族典籍翻译与研究事业关乎国家的稳定统一，关乎民族关系的和谐发展，关乎世界多元文化的实现。在中国，民族典籍资源极为丰富，有待进一步挖掘、翻译，仍有许多少数民族典籍亟待拯救，民族典籍翻译与研究工作任重而道远，民族典籍翻译事业大有可为。

李正栓①

2019 年 7 月 19 日

———————

① 李正栓，中国英汉语比较研究会典籍英译专业委员会常务副会长兼秘书长；中国中医药研究促进会传统文化翻译与国际传播专业委员会常务主任委员。

前　　言

　　《娥并与桑洛》是一部傣族叙事长诗，优美生动，凄美绝伦。1953年开始整理，1960年2月出版，1962年其同名戏剧规模演出引起轰动，被誉为"东南亚的明珠"。千百年来，它广泛流传于云南德宏、西双版纳、耿马等傣族聚居区，在傣族人民中家喻户晓，影响深远。

　　《娥并与桑洛》以朴素的形式、浪漫的情调，讲述了在封建包办婚姻制度下一对傣族青年男女的爱情悲剧，在猛烈抨击旧制度对纯真爱情戕害的同时，也热情歌颂了娥并与桑洛为争取爱情自由而勇于反抗的叛逆精神，进而成为傣族人民的愿望、感情和美好理想的寄托。

　　《娥并与桑洛》继承了傣族传统文学中叙事与抒情交融的艺术特点，充分运用傣族文学中的独特表现手法，如比喻、夸张、比兴等，语言优美含蓄，人物栩栩如生，情节有血有肉。老舍在《读了〈娥并与桑洛〉》一文中评论道："它是具有一种魅力，使人爱不释手的作品。它既不用故作惊人之笔，又不平铺直叙。它像一湖春水，反映着天上的云峰变幻。"

　　本次翻译原文选自"云南省民族民间文学德宏调查队"整理的"云南民族民间文学典藏"丛书之《娥并与桑洛》，是云南人民出版社于2009年4月第1版第1次印刷的版本。全书共98页，6万字，分为十三章。

　　在翻译过程中，译者对长诗的语言形式与文本内容进行了深刻理解与领会，以极简的翻译方法，尊重原作者的文学素养与品位，尽量还原长诗的语言特色与文化韵味；同时，译者还通过田野调查、地区走访等形式，对长诗中的人文氛围和精神环境等方面进行体验与揣摩，并以此为基础，对译本的情感把握、氛围把握与精神把握等层面进行了深入探讨。

随着"中国文化走出去"等文化方针的实施，《娥并与桑洛》等少数民族文学典籍翻译无疑对中国文化的复兴、传播与影响将产生积极的推动作用。希望此项译作能在"中国文学走出去"的道路上实实在在地往前跨一步，让外国民众通过文学审美来感受中国的魅力、增进对中国的了解、深化对中国的认识，为中国文学，包括中国少数民族文学，在世界文学中日益凸显其重要作用而贡献微薄的力量。

2019 年 7 月

目　　录

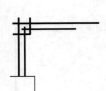

Contents

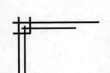

我要把这个古老的故事，
像红烛一样来点亮，
让它的光芒射到四方……

一

景多昂是个热闹的地方：
赶街的人来来往往，
牛马成群结队，
牛脖子上挂着铃铛。

景多昂是个快乐的地方：
到处是象脚鼓的声响，

Like lighting a red candle,
I would like to tell an ancient story
and let its light shine upon everything...

1

Jingduo'ang① was a lively place, full of hustle and bustle:

fair-goers coming and going,

cattle and horses moving in herds or in lines,

and bells hanging like pendants worn around the necks of the cattle.

Jingduo'ang was a happy place:

the beats of Xiangjiaogu② sounding everywhere,

the tunes of Kouxianqin③ fluttering from the bamboo huts④,

---

① Jingduo'ang is a local village in Yunnan province which is in southwest of China and comprises 8 Ethnic Minority Autonomous Regions inhabited by the vast majority of ethnic groups.

② Xiangjiaogu is a drum shaped like an elephant foot and one of the folk musical instruments in Yunnan.

③ Kouxianqin is a jaw harp with one or two metal reeds, blown by the player, and one of the folk musical instruments in Yunnan.

④ The bamboo hut is a house style of the Dai ethnic minority in Yunnan. It's built with bamboos and consists of two floors, with the higher floor for people to live in and the lower floor for pets, chicken, livestock and cattle.

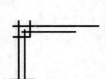

口弦在竹楼上弹奏，
琴声在竹林里飘荡。

景多昂四面都是高山，
泉水在山间流淌，
竹楼长排成行，
楼角指着星星和月亮。

广阔的田坝，
平坦得像蝴蝶的翅膀，
一直伸到高高的金塔下，
这里住着沙铁苏定那。

沙铁的钱多得像谷子，
金子银子堆得像小山，
沙铁的家漂亮又宽广，
养着成群的牛马和大象。

and the resonance of music floating in the forests.

Jingduo'ang was a mountainous place,

creeks winding through mountains,

bamboo huts lining up next to each other,

and the end of the rafter curving up① to point at the stars

and the moon.

The wide fields,

flat as the wings of the butterflies,

stretched all the way to the foot of a high Golden Tower②,

where lived a Shatie③ named Sudingna.

Shatie's money was like heaps of grain,

his gold and silver piled up like mountains,

his house was exquisite and spacious,

and he had herds of cattle, horses and elephants④.

---

①　The end of the rafter usually curves up in the shape of an egret's wing, which can be seen everywhere in the Dai area.

②　The Golden Tower is the crystal of Buddhism and the Dai people's collective wisdom, also the symbol of Dai ethnic minority and the holy place of the Dai people.

③　Shaitie refers to the richest man in the village.

④　Elephants are considered the symbol of harvest, good luck and happiness in the Dai culture, so the Chief of a Dai tribe usually keeps elephants as their pets to show their wealth and status.

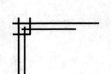

沙铁没有儿女，
夫妻成天焦虑，
这么多的财产，
死后谁来承继？

沙铁不管天晴下雨，
天天拿上鲜花，
到奘房去拜佛，
一年之后终于生了一个儿子。

沙铁夫妇高兴得不得了，
给儿子取名叫埃果那，
埃果那只活了一个月就死了，
夫妇俩哭得声音嘎哑。

过了一年又生了一个儿子，
亲戚朋友都来祝贺，

Shatie had no heir,

so he and his wife were anxious

about who would inherit

all of their assets after their death①?

Rain or shine, therefore, Shatie,

with fresh flowers in hands②,

went to pray to the Buddha everyday at the Zangfang③.

Till a year later they gave birth to a son.

The couple was thrilled

and named him Ai'guona.

But Ai'guona lived only for a month,

and the couple cried their voice hoarse.

They had another son a year later,

and the friends and the elatives all came to congratulate them

---

① The Dai ethnic minority is a matrilineal society, in which daughters have the right of inheritance.

② It's common for the Dai people to pray to the Buddha in temples on holidays, on big days or for great events.

③ Zangfang, a temple of Hīnayāna (a form of Buddhism), can be found everywhere in the Dai area, for the Dai people have great faith in Buddhism. Besides a religious place where Buddhist sermons are given and Buddhist scholars are produced, it is also a library where precious books are stored, a school where local children receive education, and a center of festival ceremonies where local and other minority culture mingle. Therefore, Zangfang is closely tied to every aspect of Dais' lives in economy, politics, culture and daily living.

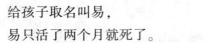

给孩子取名叫易，
易只活了两个月就死了。

夫妇俩一天到晚地悲伤，
日夜盼望再生一个孩子。
一天，沙铁的妻子做了一个梦，
梦见天上飞满星星。

一颗最明亮的星掉了下来，
落在她手上闪闪发光，
所有的亲戚朋友都跑来看望，
她忙把星星往裙子里藏。

正藏着猛然惊醒，
发现自己躺在床上。
鸡叫了，天亮了，
她把梦告诉了丈夫。

她疑惑地问：
"多么奇怪的梦啊！
快告诉我吧，
这是好事还是灾祸？"

沙铁说这是一个好梦，
他轻快得像被风吹起的树叶，
天天想抱上又白又胖的孩子，
他的妻子不久果然又怀了孕。

and named the child Yi.
But Yi lived for only two months.

The couple was grief-stricken day in and day out,
pining for another child.
One night Shatie's wife had a dream,
and she dreamt about the stars flying all over the sky.

From the sky, the brightest star fell,
twinkling and glistening right into her hands.
All the friends and relatives came to visit her,
so hurriedly she tried to hide the fallen star under her dress.

While trying, she suddenly woke up
and then realized that she was on her own bed.
When the roosters crowed and the daybreak arrived,
she told her dream to her husband.

Confounded, she exclaimed:
"What an odd dream!
Please tell me quickly,
is this a good sign or a bad one?"

Shatie said it was a good dream,
feeling such delight that he felt like a leaf flying in the air,
longing to hold a beautiful white and fat baby in his arms,
and indeed his wife was pregnant again soon.

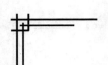

傣历三月初三，
月亮弯得像把梳子，
星星闪得特别明亮，
孩子就在这晚出世。

孩子的皮肤白得像水晶，
脸儿团团像月亮，
小嘴红得像紫椒，
父亲给他取名叫桑洛。

母亲把他抱在怀里，
喂他银白的奶，
父亲把他背在背上，
用的是绸缎的背带。

远远近近的亲戚，
姑爹姑妈舅舅，
大姐姨妈老表，
都来把桑洛称赞。

The night of March 3rd. in the Dai calendar①,
with the curvy moon in the shape of a comb
and the stars especially bright in the sky,
a boy was born into this world.

The child's skin was clear as crystal,
the face was round as the moon,
and the lips were as red as the purple peppers.
Dad Shatie named the child Sangluo.

His mother held him tightly in her arms
and fed him her silvery milk.
His father carried him on the back
and used only the silky belt②.

Relatives from near and far,
uncles and aunts,
sisters and cousins,
were all proud of Sangluo.

---

① March 3rd. in the Dai calendar is around December in the Chinese lunar calendar and February in the solar calendar. It's also the water-sprinkling festival in Dai's tradition, which symbolizes the beginning of a new year.

② It's Dai's custom to carry the baby on an adult's back with belts to secure the baby, for it's convenient for adults to do the housework and take care of the baby at the same time. The ordinary people use the belt made of rough cloth, and the Shatie (the rich people) use the silk belt.

11

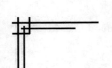

景多昂的姑娘都来了，
小玉、小安、小娥，
争着来抱桑洛，
嘴里夸奖心里羡慕：

"小桑洛呀！
你小小的就这么漂亮，
长大了更没有人比得上；
你像迎春花一样开放，
我们已被太阳晒得枯黄。

"小桑洛啊！
你生得太迟了，
我们不能采一个园子里的花，
我们不能唱一样的歌。

"小桑洛呀！
假如你是园里的花朵，
我们要把你戴在头上，
我们要把你揣在怀里。

"可惜我们相差太远，
好像大刀和斧头。
你快快长大吧！
我们闻闻香味就够了。

All the young women around Jingduo'ang came,

Xiaoyu, Xiao'an and Xiao'e,

and they could not wait for their turn to hold Sangluo,

with complimenting words and fond hearts.

"Oh, little Sangluo!

You are so little and are already so matchlessly handsome

that when you grow up you will have no equal;

you are blooming like the primroses in early Spring,

while we are already withered by the sun."

"Ah, little Sangluo!

You are born too late

to pick the flowers from the same garden as we

and to sing songs of the same kinds.①"

"Oh, little Sangluo!

If you were a blossom in the garden,

we would like to wear you on our heads

and hold you close to our hearts."

"It's a pity that there is such a difference in our ages,

like that between an machete and an axe.

Please grow up quickly!

We will be happy just to smell the fragrance of your youth."

---

① The young women in Dai usually hang out with their beloved in gardens, and sing songs to each other to show their love.

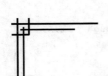

"不同辈的桑洛呀！
要是你早点生下，
我们要在竹楼下纺纱，
陪着你谈笑在月光下。"

就像一棵竹笋，
生长在绿茵茵的竹林里；
桑洛长得美丽，
逗得所有的姑娘欢喜。

就像荷花开在水池里，
走过的人都把他称赞；
都想在水边停留，
把它摘下带在自己身边。

"Little Sangluo of a different generation!

If you were born earlier,

we would have spun linen together outside of the bamboo huts①

and accompanied you chatting and laughing away under the moonlight."

Like a bamboo shoot②

in the midst of the verdant bamboo grove,

Sangluo grew to be a handsome young man

of whom all the young women were fond of.

Like a lotus flower③ in the pond,

he made all passers-by would appreciate him,

would like to stop by the pond

and would wish to pick it up and keep it to themselves.

---

① The young women in Dai usually do spinning and wait for their beloved outside of the bamboo huts at the same time.

② The bamboo shoot is a local food in Dai, and also the typical symbol of Dai.

③ The lotus flower has profound significance in the Chinese culture, especially in Dai's culture. It stands for pureness, youth, love and happiness, which were derived from Buddhism in ancient India.

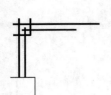

二

日子一天天过去，
日子一月月又来，
桑洛学会在地上爬，
有时爬到谷仓里去。

七月的时候父亲死了。
母亲整天哭哭啼啼。
她把丈夫埋葬，
靠儿子来解除悲伤。

桑洛一天天长大，
长到三四岁，
他在天井里跑来跑去，
有时候一个人跑出大门。

很快长到十四五岁，
桑洛成了小伙子，
天一亮就离开家，
骑着马到田野里去奔跑。

2

Days passed by one after another,
and months came one after another.
Sangluo learnt how to crawl,
sometimes even into the granary.

When he was seven months old, his father died.
His mother was weeping and sobbing all day long.
After burying her husband,
she counted on her son for some relief from her sadness.

Day by day grew up Sangluo gradually.
By the time he was three or four,
he kept running here and there in the courtyard,
sometimes even out of the gate.

Quickly turning to be an early teenager,
Sangluo became a young man,
who left home at dawn
to ride a horse that galloped in the wild field①.

---

① Galloping on the horseback is what the Dai young men usually do
in their leisure time.

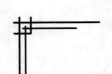

太阳落山他才回家，
拴好马又背上了琴。
他弹琴就像讲话，
他讲话也像弹琴。

人人都想和他讲话，
人人都想听他弹琴，
老人孩子爱听，
姑娘们更爱听。

姑娘们天天盼望桑洛，
天天等着桑洛的琴声，
"只要桑洛到了我家，
我马上搬凳子给他坐下。"

有的姑娘早已摆好凳子，
有的姑娘整夜在竹楼下织布，
有的靠在门边等待，

As soon as he returned home at sunset,
he hitched the horse to the post and picked up his qin①.
He played the qin as if he was talking
and he talked as if he were playing the qin.

Everyone liked to talk with him
and enjoyed listening to his playing,
the elderly, the children,
and especially the young women.

Every day the young women looked forward to Sangluo's coming,
and every day they waited for Sangluo's playing:
"If Sangluo comes to my house,
I immediately find a good stool for him to sit on②."

But others had already prepared the stool,
still others kept weaving③ in the bamboo hut all night long,
some waited leaning against the door frame

---

①　Qin, one of the traditional folk musical instruments, is made of bamboo and strings. It's widely played by the Dai young men to express their deep feelings for the young women.

②　It's a Dai's custom for the young women to prepare good stools for the most popular guys, and the bad stools for the unpopular ones.

③　It's a Dai's custom for the young women to learn weaving by using the looms. They weave the cloth and do the embroidery for their wedding dresses all by themselves for several years, starting when they are teenagers.

19

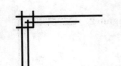

有的拿锄头去修好门前的路。

有的姑娘听说桑洛要来，
把竹门换成新的；
有的姑娘听说桑洛要来，
拿一根竹棍到楼边去吆狗。

景多昂的姑娘，
天不亮就忙着去挑水，
井边的水桶在碰撞，
挑水的姑娘一行行。

为了看看桑洛，
挑水的姑娘，
故意从他家门前绕过，
桑洛的门前姑娘多，水桶也多。

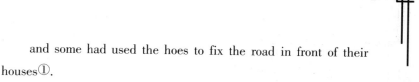

and some had used the hoes to fix the road in front of their houses①.

On hearing that Sangluo would come,

some changed the bamboo gate into a new one②.

On hearing that Sangluo would come,

and some even used a bamboo stick to scare the dogs away③.

The young women in Jingduo'ang

were busy carrying the water from wells④ before dawn,

so the water buckets clacking by the well,

and line after line were the young women carrying the water.

In order to have a look at Sangluo,

they detoured on purpose

so that they could walk in front of his house.

There were many young women and water buckets in front of his house.

---

① The roads in the Dai area are usually the earthen ones full of pits and holes, so it's necessary to fix them especially for the distinguished figures, or on big days.

② The bamboo gate is often dampened and therefore easily rotten, so it's usually changed into a new one on big days.

③ The Dai young women usually scare away the dogs outside the gates especially for the honored guests.

④ In Dai's culture, men never do housework like carrying water or cooking, while women do that. Women usually carry water in buckets from wells or rivers quite early in the morning.

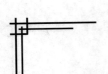

桑洛长大了，
姑娘们对他更是喜欢，
老年人说桑洛是自家的亲戚，
姑娘们说桑洛是妈妈的女婿。

桑洛从寨子走过，
姑娘们都把窗子打开，
心里的话呀，
不好意思说出口来。

"桑洛哥哥呀！
假如你是一朵花，
我要睡在你的花瓣下，
夜晚闻着你的芳香，
早晨看着你开放。"

"桑洛哥哥呀！
你要是一只燕子，
就请到我家来搭窝。
我家的屋梁最干净，
哪管你只借宿几天，
我都会喜欢得掉泪。"

Sangluo had grown up,

and the young women were fond of him even more.

The elderly said that Sangluo was related to them,

and young women said that Sangluo was their mother's son-

in-law.

When Sangluo was passing a village,

young women there would open all the windows,

but too shy to say

what they really wanted to say to him.

"Big brother①, Sangluo!

If you were a flower,

I would like to sleep under your petals,

enjoying your fragrance at night

and watching you to blossom at dawn."

"Big brother, Sangluo!

If you were a swallow,

please build your nest near my house.

My eaves are cleanest.

Even if you would stay for only a few days,

I will be so happy that I will shed tears!"

---

①　Big brother doesn't mean a family member. It's Dai's custom to call
a young man older in age or being loved by young women.

小玉姑娘心里更着急，
她梳光了头发，
学当新媳妇。
一个人在屋里扭来扭去，
一不小心跌在门槛上，
碰肿了膝头。

安毕昂姑娘高高兴兴，
说妈妈就要把她嫁给桑洛，
结婚的事不用愁，
只愁出嫁那天怎样打扮。

阿佐姑娘早已戴上耳环，
套上漂亮的手镯，
把小凳子背在背上，
学妈妈哄娃娃。

本寨的姑娘爱桑洛，
外寨的姑娘也爱桑洛，
母亲一个也不选，
偏偏选了阿扁或安佐。

The young woman, Xiaoyu, was anxious
that she dressed her hair slick①
and behaved like a new bride,
wiggling her hips as she walked.
In a moment of carelessness, she tripped over the threshold,
and her knees swelling up.

The young woman, Anbi'ang, was also excited
to claim that her mother had agreed to her marriage to San-
gluo②,
so she didn't need to worry about her marriage,
but how to dress-up and makeup on her big day.

The young woman, A'zuo, had long been wearing earrings
and beautiful bracelets,
carrying a small stool on her back③,
imitating a new mum teasing her baby.

Many young women in Jingduo'ang loved Sangluo,
and many young women outside of it loved him too,
yet his mother chose none of them
but A'bian or An'zuo.

---

① The Dai young women are fond of growing their hair long. They usually tie it up into a bun with flowers, combs, scarves, high hats or bamboo leaf hats.

② The marriage in Dai's culture is usually arranged by parents according to their social status or ranks.

③ The Dai young women usually carry a stool along with them for their beloved to sit down anytime and anywhere they meet them.

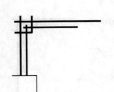

三

离景多昂不远，
有个景算地方，
这里也有一家沙铁，
这家是桑洛的姨妈。

桑洛的姨妈，
有两个女儿，
一个叫阿扁，
一个叫安佐。

阿扁鼻子高高的，
长得又白又细，
她常到桑洛家来玩，
总是讨得桑洛母亲的欢喜。

阿扁好像一条蛇，
在桑洛身边扭来扭去，
就是桑洛的影子，
她也要追随。

3

Not far from Jingduo'ang
was Jingsuan,
where there was also a Shatie,
the family of Sangluo's aunt, his mother's sister.

Sangluo's aunt
had two daughters,
and their names were A'bian
and A'zuo.

A'bian had a high nose,
beautiful white skin and a delicate stature.
She visited Sangluo's family frequently
and always won his mother's favor.

A'bian was like a snake,
slithering her way around Sangluo,
even if it were just his shadow,
she would keep purchasing it.

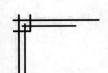

她有换不完的新衣服，
她有戴不完的花藤圈，
嘴里叫着"咪叭，咪叭"，
心里想做人家的媳妇。

她脚上的藤圈，
有绳子一样粗。
她嘴里讲的，
都是别家姑娘的坏处。
她头上天天戴花，
多得发髻也插不下。
看见男人口水特别多，
走路也要扯扯裙子和衣角。

安佐也整天跟着桑洛转，
脸上的粉搽得像灰猫，
头发上扭得出油来，
天天请人写情书给桑洛。

安佐与阿扁，
就像起了锈的黄铜，

28

She had countless new clothes to change

and endless flora rattans① to wear,

calling Sangluo's mother "mi ba, mi ba"②,

but wanting to be her daughter-in-law.

The flora rattans on her ankles

were as thick as ropes.

The words out of her mouth

were always something ill about other young women.

The flowers on her head

were too many for other hair accessories.

She drooled over any men,

and always pulled her skirt or the corner of her blouse even

when walking.

Nor would A'zuo leave Sangluo alone for any minute,

everyday wearing too much rouge that she looked like a gray

cat,

too much grease in her hair that you could wring oil out of it,

and every day she asked others to write love letters to San-

gluo for her.

A'zuo and A'bian

were like rusty bronze,

---

① Flora rattans are the Dai young women's accessories on feet,
black, slim and bright.

② Mi ba means "mother" in Dai's dialect.

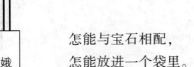
怎能与宝石相配，
怎能放进一个袋里。

这样的姑娘，
母亲偏偏欢喜，
母亲要桑洛
挑选一个做妻子。

听说桑洛母亲喜欢阿扁、安佐，
阿扁的母亲，
走起路来洋洋得意，
踩在狗尾巴上也不觉得。

每天她到桑洛家几次，
送来桑洛喜欢的东西。
母亲连忙把东西放进柜里，
桑洛看也不看一眼。

母亲要桑洛娶阿扁，
说阿扁是他家的亲戚，
整天的唠叨纠缠，
桑洛心里很厌烦：

how could they be of any match for the precious jewel
and how would it be possible for them to be put in the same
bag with it.

But there were such kinds of young women
his mother liked
and between them
his mother asked him to choose one as his wife①.

Upon hearing that Sangluo's mother liked A'bian and A'zuo,
A'bian's mother
was so pleased with herself
that she could not feel anything even when stepping onto a
dog tail.

She visited Sangluo several times a day
to bring him his favorite things,
which his mother immediately stored away
but Sangluo did not even look at.

Sangluo's mother wanted Sangluo to marry A'bian,
because A'bian was their relative.
So constant and insistent was his mother
that Sangluo became rather annoyed.

---

　① It was widely common for the Dai people to look for their spouses
among the relatives in the ancient time which led to many drawbacks in Dai's
population.

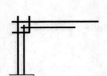

"可爱的姑娘走在水上，
水也不会动荡；
阿扁走在地上，
竹楼都会摇晃。

"人家说，
刺都戳不痛她的脚，
她一走进花园啊，
嫩苗都要遭殃。

"她织的布，
像一朵枯萎的花，
就是她织出十朵花，
我也不会爱她。"

"Not even a single ripple is caused
when a lovely young women walks on the water,
but bamboo huts shake
when A'bian walks by."

"It's said that
A'bian feels no pain, even when thorns poke her feet,
and as soon as she enters a garden,
the disaster for all tender buds has arrived."

"The cloth she weaves
is like a withered flower①.
I won't love her
even if she weaves ten such flowers."

---

① The Dai young women learn the cloth-weaving at an early age and make their gorgeous wedding dresses out of the cloth weaved and dyed all by themselves. Those who are good at weaving and dyeing are considered "good girls / wives" who will marry better men, but those who are not good at weaving and dyeing are seen as "non-virtuous girls/ wives" who will hardly get married.

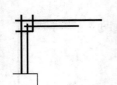
四

一枝花谢了，
一枝花又接着开，
桑洛的故事永远讲不完，
像月亮落下，
第二天又升起来。

景多昂很热闹，
做生意的人来来往往，
牛群叮当的铃声四处响，
桑洛的心飞向远方。

他向母亲请求，
让他出门做生意，
他愿像牛群走遍山林，
不愿像宝石关锁在柜里。

母亲听了儿子的话，
千言万语阻挡他：
"心爱的桑洛呀！
你天天和我在一起，
你像我的镜子，
我一天也离不开你。

4

One flower withers,
yet another one will bloom,
just like Sangluo's story will never end,
just like the moon sets,
but will rise again the next day.

Jingduo'ang was as lively as ever,
with businessmen coming and going,
cattle's bells ringing everywhere
and Sangluo's heart flew afar.

He begged his mother
to let him leave home to do business,
for he would rather be like a cattle travelling around a wider
forest
than be like a precious diamond locked in the cabinet.

On hearing his son's pleading,
his mother used her own words to stop him:
"My dear Sangluo!
We are together every day
like me and my mirror;
I can't live without you."

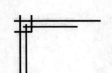

"家里有的是金银，
你怎么想到做生意？
家里有这么多牛马，
你怎么不骑？
家乡有那么多姑娘爱你，
你怎么不娶？

"我的儿子呀！
我爱你哟，
像爱勐欢的宝石，
你快不要这样想，
做生意是辛苦的事。"

桑洛越想越苦恼：
"我像一只小鸟被关在笼里，
只能低着头淌眼泪，
不能像鹦哥到山里去飞。

"我只想走进深山老林，
自由自在地满山跑，
可惜不能随我的心！
我像一只大象，
被人紧紧地关在屋里。"

"There is an abundance of gold and silver in our home.

What on earth lures you into the idea of doing business?

There are numerous horses and cattle in our home.

Why don't you just ride them?

There are so many young women loving you in our hometown.

Why don't you marry any one of them?"

"My son!

I love you

as I do the jewels from Menghuan①.

Give up on the thought,

for doing business is rather hard."

The more Sangluo thought about this, the more distressed he became:

"I'm like a bird locked in a cage,

can but weep with my head down,

cannot fly like a parrot into the forest."

"I only long for deep mountains and ancient forests,

running freely and randomly as I like,

but I cannot follow my heart right now!

Like an elephant in captivity,

I'm stuck in this house."

---

①　Menghuan is a village in the Dai area.

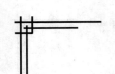

桑洛天天要求出去，
他用温和的语言，
向母亲苦苦请求，
母亲不得不同意。
桑洛就像脱了缰的马，
去把朋友们约齐。

景多昂的小伙子，
个个愿和桑洛在一起，
听说要到外地去，
没有一个不愿意。

大家把衣服装进箱子，
拉来黄牛装好驮子。
换上新的绳，
装好吃的米。

牛驮子一排排放好，
桑洛要出发了。
他打扮得真漂亮，
银色的长刀背在背上。

桑洛脸上闪着红光，
头上戴着三角篾帽，

Every day Sangluo begged for his freedom,
in gentle words pleading with his mother,
who finally relented.
Sangluo, feeling like a horse that was finally free,
started planning with all his friends.

Every young man in Jingduo'ang
liked to be with Sangluo.
On hearing about the new journey,
none turned down the idea.

They packed their clothes,
loaded them onto the yellow cattle,
changed the new ropes
and prepared the delicious rice.

With the cattle all lined up,
Sangluo was ready to set out.
He looked gorgeous,
with a long silver machete on his back①.

His face was radiant
under a triangular bamboo hat②,

---

①　The long machete in Dai is usually for men's daily working and personal safety, which is derived from the short knife used in daily working.

②　A bamboo hut is made of thin slices of bamboo, usually in the shape of trigonometric cone, with three corners at the brim flying in curves.

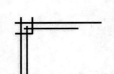

太阳照着他的衣裳，
金色的纽扣也在闪光。

桑洛的马也很俊美，
脖子上的铃叮叮当当。
桑洛高高骑在马上，
金线绣的鞋子踏在镫上。

景多昂的姑娘穿得漂漂亮亮，
站在路旁送桑洛，
看见桑洛走过，
姑娘们唱起了歌：
"多好的桑洛哥哥呀！
你为什么要离开家乡？

"我们的地方这样好，
你为什么想到远方？
我们从小一起长大，
难道你的爱情呵，
要到远方去寻找？

"桑洛哥哥呀！
你像高高树梢上的一朵花，
我们这些姑娘啊，
只能抬着头白白地望着它。

with the golden buttons
of his shirt glistening in the sunshine!

His horse was a fine one,
wearing the bells on its neck;
on the tall steed was Sangluo,
with the gold-thread embroidered boots glittering on the stir-
rups!

All the young women in Jingduo'ang dressed up
to see him off by the roadsides,
singing upon his passing-by①:
"Oh, our lovely big brother Sangluo!
Why do you want to leave your home town? "

"Why do you want to go far away
from such a good place like ours?
We grew up together,
but must you look for your love
from faraway places?"

"Oh, big brother Sangluo!
You are like a flower, blooming so high in a big tree
that we young women
could but raise our heads, yearning in vain."

①　The Dai people are good at expressing their emotions and feelings
by singing. They sing in nearly every situation such as working, relaxing,
praying and memorizing.

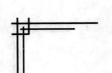

"桑洛哥哥呀！
你不喜欢家乡，
你不喜欢我们，
就像森林里的小鸟，
尝到苦味的野果，
慌忙从森林里飞走了。

"墙外的金银花呀！
我们天天想把你摘下；
戴在我们头上。
现在永远不能够了，
蜜蜂蝴蝶把花采走了。

"亲爱的桑洛哥哥，
你要离开我们，
就像水鸭子
不愿走进陌生的池塘。

"你像深山里的麂子，
挣断了猎人的缰绳，
飞快地跑进森林，
到更远的山里去了。

"Oh, big brother Sangluo!
You like not our hometown
and not us,
but you are like a forest bird,
on tasting the bitter wild berries,
hurriedly taking its leave from the forest."

"The golden and silvery honeysuckles outside of the walls!
Every day we dream about picking you
and wearing you on our heads.
Now can we never do so any more,
because you have been picked by bees and butterflies."

"Dear big brother Sangluo,
you are leaving us
like a duck
avoiding an unfamiliar pond."

"You are like a mountain deer,
having freed itself from a hunter's bondage,
galloping into a forest
and towards another mountain afar."

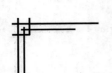

"漂亮的哥哥呀！
姑娘们的心，
像干池塘里的青蛙，
盼望着大雨快快淋下。
愿你不要忘记了家乡，
不要永远在外面流浪。

"桑洛哥哥呀！
你要离开家乡，
我们只能送点槟榔，
嚼着槟榔你就会想起我们。

"我们想念你，
我们等待你，
不要让粉红的花朵枯萎，
不要让新绣的金花褪色。
要是不怕爹妈骂，
我们一定跟着你去。

"去吧！我们无法把你拉住，
我们挡不住你的路，
只求你好好记住我们的话，
记住我们的祝福。

"Oh, handsome big brother!
The hearts of us young women
are like frogs in a dry pond,
longing for a heavy rain.
Hope that you will never forget your hometown
and do not wander in the alien land forever."

"Oh, big brother Sangluo!
You want to leave your hometown,
and we can but give you some areca nuts① as a gift
to remember us when you chew them."

"We will miss you
and await you!
Please don't let pink flowers wither,
or newly embroidered golden flowers fade.
If it were not for fear of our parents' threatening words,
we would definitely accompany you."

"Go! We can't stop you from leaving
or block your path,
so we plead with you to remember our words
and our good wishes."

---

① The Dai people have the habit of chewing areca nuts in their leisure time, for it is considered good for both teeth and body.

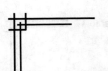

"去吧，慢慢地走吧！
不要忧愁，不要牵挂。
愿你高高兴兴地去，
愿你高高兴兴地回家。

"要是你能活一千年，
一千年也不要忘记我们；
你就是走得再远，
我们也在你身边。

"去吧！快快地去吧！
快快地回来吧！
发光的宝石啊，
不要让银盒子空着。"

姑娘们举手把槟榔、茶叶
递给桑洛，
露出了雪白的手臂、
银亮的手镯。

姑娘们的话，
好像森林里的鸟儿叫，
叫开了岩石上的花，
桑洛高兴地回答：

"Go and walk slowly①!
Have no worry or concern.
We wish you a happy journey
and a happy homecoming."

"If you live a thousand years,
don't forget us for that long;
no matter how far away you travel,
we will always be there by your side!"

"Go! Go quickly!
And come back quickly!
Ah, you the shiny sapphire,
please do not let the silver box here be empty."

The young women handed areca nuts and tea
to Sangluo,
their white forearms
and silver bracelets showing.

The young women's words
were like birds' tweeting in the forest
that opened up flowers on rocks.
Sangluo replied with delight:

---

① It's Dai's way to show politeness when seeing someone off, and wish him safety all his way along.

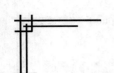

"再见了，姑娘们！
我们要走了，
并不是为了离开你们，
并不是因为不爱家乡。

"亲爱的姑娘们！
愿你们在家里，
打扮得更漂亮，
歌唱得更响亮。

"姑娘们啊！你们像孔雀一样，
孔雀的美在它的羽毛上；
你们像龙银鸟一样，
龙银鸟的美在它的声音上；
你们像公鸡一样，
公鸡的美在它长长的尾巴上；
姑娘们啊！你们的美，
是在你们的心上。

"宝石一样的姑娘们啊！
我永远记着你们，
永远不会把你们遗忘。
树林里鸟叫的时候，
我就会想起你们；
田里开始插秧的时候，

"So long, young women!
We are about to depart
but not because of you,
nor because we love not our hometown."

"Dear young women!
While you stay at home,
I hope that you make yourself even more beautiful
and sing songs even more resoundingly!"

"Ah, young women!
Like peacocks① whose beauty are their colorful feathers,
like Longyin birds② whose loveliness is their tuneful tweeting,
and like roosters whose elegance are their fancy tails;
ah, young women! Your beauty
are your hearts."

"Ah, jewel-like young women!
I will always remember you
and never forget you.
Every time birds tweet in the forest,
I will remember you;
by the season of rice transplanting next year,

---

①　Peacock is also called the sun bird, which is the symbol of good
luck, happiness and love in Dai's culture.
②　Longyin bird is a local bird in Dai.

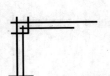
我就会回到家乡。"

桑洛骑在马上，
转回头向姑娘们招手，
铃子的声音渐渐消失，
离家的人们走远了……

I will return to our hometown."

Riding the horse,

Sangluo turned his head back and waved to the young women,

sound of the bell gradually vanished

and the young men who left their hometown rode into distance...

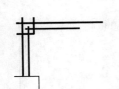

五

天竹长大了，
笋叶一张张掉在地上。
我的歌啊！
像露水淋湿的树枝，
又发出了嫩绿的芽。

离开了景多昂，
牛铃叮叮当当地响，
牛在呜哦呜哦地叫，
吆牛的小伙子心里也高兴，
在树林里唱起了山歌。

走过竹林，
又走进森林，
遇见挡路的刺丛，
用长刀把它们斩尽。

走了一整天，
太阳落山了，
桑洛和他的朋友们，
卸下牛驮子，
要在森林里住宿。

5

The bamboo has grown up,
and its bamboo leaves have fallen to the ground one after an-
other.
Ah, my song!
It is like a twig, moist with dew,
giving out tender and green sprouts again.

Having left Jingduo'ang
and listening to the cattle mooing with their bells ringing,
Sangluo was rather happy deep inside
and started to sing folk songs.

Having just gone through the bamboo groves,
they entered forests,
using their long machetes to cut thorns and brambles
that came their way.

At sunset
and after marching a whole day,
Sangluo and his friends
unloaded the cattle
and started the camps in a forest.

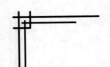

有的放牛去吃草，
有的上山去找柴，
有的泉边去淘米，
熊熊的篝火烧起来。

深山的夜，
特别美丽，
月亮忽儿被树梢遮住，
忽儿又从林中露出。

月亮的光照在大地上，
照在密密的树林里，
四周静悄悄，
只有小鸟在咕咕咕地叫。

月亮又露出来了，
清凉的霜落在人们脸上，
桑洛的琴声轻轻飘起，
他歌唱可爱的家乡。

他想起门前的水井，
每天早上挤满了水桶，
挑水的姑娘们，
这时该起床了……

Some of them went to tend cattle on the pasture,
others went to collect firewood on the hills,
still others went to wash rice by the spring,
and the roaring bonfires were then started.

The night deep in the mountains
was especially beautiful,
and the moon veiled itself behind the treetops for a moment
but unveiled itself from the branches for another.

The moonlight shone upon the land,
upon the thick forest,
quietly and silently,
with only the sound of little birds cooing lightly.

When the moon appeared again,
and cool frost fell on their faces,
the sound of Sangluo's qin was wafting in the air,
and he was singing a song of his lovely hometown.

He remembered the well-water in front of his house,
crowed with lines of buckets every morning,
and the young women carrying water,
should have got up then...

天蒙蒙亮，
风吹树叶哗哗响，
野鸡在山谷里啼叫，
小伙子们起身了。

没有出过门的黄牛，
走得很慢很慢，
小伙子抽了一鞭，
它又蹦蹦跳跳跑上前。

离开景多昂很远了，
又来到一个村寨。
这里的姑娘嘴是甜的，
跑来向客人问长问短：

"哥哥们从哪里来？
要到哪里去？
你们的牛真多啊，
你们牛的铃子真响啊。

"你们来到这里，
好像月亮升在天边，
可惜我们之间啊，
像太阳和月亮一样离得远。"

At dawn,

with the wind whistling through leaves

and pheasants crowing in the valley,

the young men set off again.

The cattle had never travelled that far from home before,

so they were moving rather slowly.

When the young men whipped them,

they hurried forward a little bit.

They were quite far away from Jingduo'ang

when they came to a village.

The young women here were good at giving compliments,

and curious about everything of their guests:

"Where are you from, big brothers?

And where are you headed?

How numerous are your cattle

and how resounding is the jingling of your cattle's bells."

"Your coming here

is like the moon rising in the horizon.

It is a pity that we are so far away from each other,

as far away as the sun and the moon are from each other."

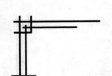

又走了一天，
天快黑了，
星星围着月亮，
乌云罩在山顶，
像一朵朵的花，
在森林上空飘动。

他们又走进一个寨子，
寨子边的水泉旁，
挑水的姑娘穿梭不停，
裙子的声音沙沙窸窸，
好像在说：
"漂亮的哥哥，
去哪里？去哪里？"

她们从泉边走来，
挑着清凉的泉水，
走得那么轻盈，
好像燕子飞。

天快亮了，
牛铃在响动。
桑洛背上了腰刀，
骑上了骏马。

经过寨边泉水旁，
穿过热闹的街子，
姑娘们向桑洛问好，
水晶的耳环摇摇晃晃。

At the end of another day's journey,
it was nearly dark,
stars scattering and twinkling around the moon,
dark clouds gathering over the mountain tops,
like floating flowers over the forest.

They entered another village
where along the stream next to the village
young women were carrying water back and forth,
their skirts rustling
as if saying:
"Handsome big brothers,
where are you going? Where are you going?"

The young women came from the spring,
with buckets of cool and fresh spring water on their shoulders
and walking gracefully and elegantly
like flying swallows.

When the daybreak was near
and cattle's bells were ringing again,
Sangluo put on his machete
and mounted his horse again.

Passing by the stream along the village
and through the lively streets in the village,
Sangluo was greeted warmly by all the young women there,
with their crystal earrings swinging and swaying.

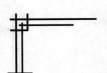

穿过一座茂密的大森林，
来到崩龙族的地方，
眼前是一片绿色的茶林，
密密层层像秧田一样。

牛的铃声传到山上，
戴着银项圈的崩龙族姑娘，
背着竹篓篓，
一齐跑下山来。

按照崩龙族的风俗，
准备了丰盛的饭菜，
招待远方来的客人，
招待漂亮的桑洛。

桑洛也回送了礼物，
送的是槟榔和烟草，
崩龙姑娘又敬献了茶叶，
邀请客人们上山休息。

He went through a dense forest
and came to an area that belonged to the Benglong ethnic mi-
nority①,
and in front of him was an area of green tea bushes,
layer upon layer like rice paddies.

The bell ringing of the cattle reached to the top of hills,
and the young Benglong women, wearing silver necklaces
and carrying bamboo back buckets②,
rushed downhill towards him.

According to Benglong's custom,
they prepared many a delicious dishes
to treat the guests from afar,
to treat handsome Sangluo.

Sangluo returned their kindness
with his gifts of areca nuts and tobacco leaves,
and the Benglong young women then offered some tea
and invited their guests to take a rest up in the mountains.

---

①　Benglong ethnic minority is one of 55 ethnic minorities in China,
which changed its name into De'ang ethnic minority in 1985.

②　The back bucket is made of bamboo strips or rattans, which is carried on one's back to hold things.

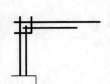
六

话儿呀说不完，
歌儿呀唱不完，
像姑娘坐在织布机前，
永远织不尽那长长的线。

走了一天又一天，
第三天来到了猛根地方。
猛根遍地是鲜花，
一朵朵盛开在地上。

猛根城里很热闹，
城外流过一条大河，
河里有起伏的波浪，
河边有美丽的姑娘。

桑洛来到猛根，
像春天的泉水，
流进了城外的大河；

6

The story is not finished
and the song does not end,
just like never-ending long thread
before those who are in front of looms.

After another two days,
they arrived at Menggen①,
where fresh flowers were everywhere
and each one was blossoming.

The Menggen village was very lively,
with a big river running by it from outside
in which were waves rising
and by which were beautiful young women.

On arriving at Menggen,
Sangluo felt like a spring water
now running into a river outside the village,

---

①　Menggen is a village in the Dai area.

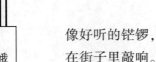

像好听的铓锣，
在街子里敲响。

牛群停在猛根的塔下，
猛根的人们都来接待客人。
姑娘打扮得像鲜花一样，
害羞地看着他们。

人们给商队找了舒适的住处，
男男女女都热情地来看望。
桑洛请人家尝了新鲜的茶叶，
客人的大方很快传到四方。

到了赶街天，
猛根城里的人真多，
都想来尝点茶叶，
都想来看看桑洛。

这样漂亮的青年，
猛根从没有见过，
猛根城热闹得像一条河，
人们像鱼一样来往穿梭。

like pleasant Mang gongs①
sounding off in the street lanes.

When their herds of cattle stopped at the bottom of a tower in
Menggen,
the people there came out and warmly greeted their guests.
The young women there dressed like fresh flowers,
looking at them shyly.

They prepared comfortable accommodations for the trading
team,
and men and women came to visit them.
Sangluo, in return, prepared fresh tea for everyone
and quite soon the generosity of the guests became well-
known in Menggen.

On the day of the fair,
many came to the village of Menggen,
everyone wanting to taste the tea
and everyone wanting to see Sangluo.

Such handsome young lad
was never seen in Menggen before.
The village was as lively as a river,
everyone walking on and by like fishes swimming at ease
back and forth.

---

①　Mang gong is also called Dong gong, Ru gong, Nai gong or Baobao
gong, which is made of bronze and in shape of a breast. It's a kind of popular
percussion instruments in many Chinese ethnic minorities.

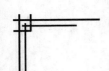

猛根的姑娘都来了，
放下了装得满满的水桶，
丢下了手里织的布，
停下了转动的纺车。

姑娘们穿着绸裙，
像水塘里的鸭子一样美丽，
嘴里嚼着槟榔，
金耳环一晃一晃。

怕羞的姑娘，
假装买东西，
慢慢从桑洛面前走过，
怕头发不好看，
一边走路一边梳头。

大胆的姑娘，
高高举着双手，
笑嘻嘻地对客人们说：
"远方的哥哥们，
我们是换东西来的。"

有的姑娘太高兴了，
把两句话也说错了：
"远方的哥哥们，
我们换你们来了。"

All the young women in Menggen came.
They put down the buckets full of water,
put away the cloth they were weaving,
and stopped their spinning wheels.

In their silk dresses,
the young women looked as beautiful as colorful ducks in
ponds,
chewing areca nuts,
with their gold earrings swinging and swaying.

Those who were too shy
pretended that they were there to shop,
passing in front of Sangluo.
For fear of their hairdo wasn't nice enough,
they combed their hair while walking by.

Those who were bolder
raised their hands,
greeting their guests and smiling:
"Dear big brothers from afar,
we come to trade merchandises with you."

Some who were overexcited
misspoke:
"Big brothers from afar,
we come to trade you."

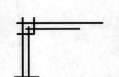
好吃的水果，
送给人们尝；
客人们的东西，
大家争着买光。

桑洛来到猛根，
像春风吹送花香……

Delicious fruits

were offered for everyone to taste,

and all the merchandises of the guests

were bought by the eager Menggeners

Sangluo's arrival at Menggen

was as refreshing as the fragrance of flowers in the Spring

breeze...

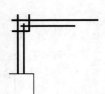
七

漂亮的花苞，
一串串垂在树上。
像鲜花一样的歌啊，快开放吧！
人们等着闻你的芳香。

猛根靠着大山，
山下有河水流过，
河水流不尽，
猛根一年四季有歌声。

古老的猛根城啊，
有个美丽的姑娘，
比棉花还要洁白，
比云彩还要柔和。

手指像竹笋，
声音像口弦，
她会说会讲，
她的名字叫娥并。

7

The pretty buds
are hanging in clusters from the tree branches.
The song as pretty as fresh flowers is blooming soon!
People are awaiting the fragrance.

Menggen was located at the bottom of a huge mountain,
where a river was running
all the year round,
so Menggen was full of sound of songs in all four seasons.

In this ancient village Menggen
lived a beautiful girl,
who was whiter than cotton,
and gentler than clouds.

Her fingers were slim like bamboo shoots,
and her voice was like that of Kouxianqin.
She was good with words,
and her name was E'bing.

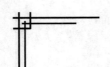

园子里的菜，
韭菜长得最快；
猛根的姑娘，
数荷花样的娥并最漂亮。

娥并的歌声又细又轻，
全寨子的人都爱听。
小伙子们听见，
再不敢拨动琴弦。

娥并听到桑洛的消息，
她停下织机，
向母亲请求：
"亲爱的妈妈，
答应我去赶街吧！
我只去一天。"

女儿要出门，
母亲不放心：
"我的姑娘啊！
你正像鲜花一样开放，
别到街上去吧！
我怕有人会把鲜花损伤。

Of the veggies in the garden,

chives grew fastest;

of the young women in Menggen,

lotus-flower-like E'bing was most beautiful.

Her voice was so tender and gentle

that everyone in this village liked to listen to.

On hearing her,

no young lad would want to pluck the strings of qin any

more.

On learning about Sangluo,

she stopped her loom and begged her mother:

"Dear Mum,

please allow me to go to the fair①!

Only one day!"

Her mother was worried

about E'bing's going out:

"My daughter!

You are right now as blooming as a blossom in the garden,

so perhaps you shouldn't go!

I'm afraid that someone will do damage to the fresh flower."

_____

①　Going to the fair is a social occasion for shopping in a certain place
after a certain period of time.

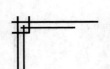

"我的姑娘啊！
你像一朵娇嫩的小花，
从小开在我的花蓬里，
我怕旁人会把你偷偷摘去。

"从前赶街，
叫你去你也不去；
今天赶街，
不叫你去偏要去。

"你是想买什么东西？
家里有你吃的，
家里有你穿的。

"你是要买口弦琴？
家里还有四五个。
每个都吹得响，
每个都吹得好听。

"你想吃水果？
园里的果子已经成熟。
你要想戴花？"
园里的花开得正鲜艳。

"心爱的娥并啊，
听妈的话吧！
街子上没有好吃的，
街子上的果子又苦又酸。"

"Ah, my daughter!
You are like a sheltered young flower,
having grown up in my greenhouse.
I'm afraid that someone will steal you away from me."

"In the past,
I asked you to go to the fair, but you wouldn't;
today,
I ask you not to go, but you insist on going."

"What do you need to buy?
There is food for you to eat
and clothes for you to wear at home."

"Do you want to buy a Kouxianqin?
There are four or five ones at home.
Everyone of them sounds clear,
and everyone is good."

"Do you want to eat fruits?
Those in the garden are ripe.
Do you want to buy flowers?
Those in the garden are at their prime."

"Ah, my beloved E'bing!
Please hear my words!
There is nothing delicious out there in the street,
and the fruits out there are bitter and sour."

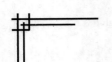

听了母亲的话，
娥并没有回答。
她脱下漂亮的衣裳，
把衣裳挂在栏杆上。

母亲看见女儿脱了衣服，
放心地走进屋里去了。
娥并悄悄地出了门，
走了很远又换了另一件衣裳。
她戴上鲜花和银手镯，
戴上闪光的金耳环，
口里嚼着槟榔，
她来到街上像仙女从天而降。

娥并稳稳地走在街子上，
她的衣裳闪闪发光。
娥并走得大大方方，
头上的花啊，
引得蜜蜂蝴蝶奔忙。

街子上的人们看见她，
想买东西的人忘了买，
想卖东西的人忘了卖；
拿着秤杆的人，
忘了把秤锤挂上；
吃饭的人放下碗，
错把菜盆端起。

On hearing her mother's words,
E'bing didn't say anything.
She took off her beautiful clothes
and hang them on the bar.①

On seeing her changing her clothes,
her mother was relieved and went back to her own room.
But E'bing sneaked out of the room,
and changed her dress again
after she had walked far away from home.
She put on some fresh flowers, the silver bracelets
and the shiny gold earrings.
Chewing areca nuts,
she descended onto the street like a fairy from the sky.

E'bing strolled in the street,
calmly and confidently,
her blouse glistening under the sunshine
and flowers on her head
attracting busy bees and butterflies.

At the sight of her,
the shoppers forgot to shop,
and the sellers forgot to sell;
those who held the weight beam forgot to hang the weights,
and those who were eating put down their rice bowls
but mistook their dishes instead.

---

① In the Dai area, the bar in the bedroom is for hanging clothes.

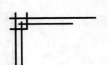

喝茶的人见了她，
往碗里丢进了烟草；
抽烟的人见了她，
烟叶掉了还不住地吸。

娥并东张西望，
到处寻找桑洛。
街子上一阵马蹄响，
桑洛和他的朋友们赶街来了。

两块远远相隔的草坪，
今天连在一起了。
娥并和桑洛，
今天相会了。

像河水流进海洋，
赶街的人都围在他们身边，
都来看美丽的娥并，
都来看漂亮的桑洛。

谁也不知道他俩的心，
他们用眼睛说话；
谁也不知道他俩的心，
就像朗并会见雪加。

At sight of her,

the tea drinkers threw the tobacco into the cup by mistake,

At sight of her,

the smokers kept smoking even if tobacco leaves had all fall-

en.

E'bing looked around,

looking for Sangluo.

Then with the clop of hoofs in the street,

Sangluo and his team arrived at the fair.

The far-away lawns

connected with each other on this day.

E'bing and Sangluo

met each other on this day.

Like rivers gathering into the sea,

people flooded the streets

to see beautiful E'bing

and to see handsome Sangluo.

None knew their hearts,

and they two connected with their eyes;

None knew their hearts,

like Langbing and Xuejia① did on meeting each other.

——————————

　　① Langbing is a fairy in the Dai folktales, and Xuejia is a god in Dai's fairytales.

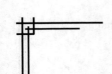

娥并和桑洛，
两颗心连在一起。
爱情呵！像金色的藤，
攀在一棵树上，
扭得比丝线还紧。

桑洛回到住的地方，
悄悄拴好了马，
急忙走到河边，
驾着小船在河里划。

娥并正站在河里洗头，
像一朵初开的荷花，
手臂像两只象牙，
小鱼在她身边游来游去。

河水哗哗地流淌，
桑洛的船在水上漂荡，
桑洛的歌声娥并听不清，
娥并望着河水轻轻地唱：

E'bing and Sangluo,

their hearts connected.

Oh, love! It was like golden vines

climbing a tree

and embracing more tightly than silk threads on the weav-

ings.

After getting back to the place,

they stayed and hitched the horse to the post,

and Sangluo hurried to the riverside,

got into a boat and kept rowing.

So happened that E'bing was washing her hair standing in the

river①,

like a lotus flower that had just bloomed,

her two arms like two ivories,

with little fish swimming around her.

With the water rustling by,

Sangluo's boat was floating in the river.

Sangluo's singing did not yet quite reach E'bing,

who was singing softly to the river②:

---

① It's Dai's custom for women to take showers or wash hair in the river, claiming that all the dirty things in or out of body can be swept off by the
river water.

② It's quite common for young men and women to sing antiphonal
songs, if they see in each other.

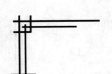

"小河呵！
你流轻一些吧，
让我听听桑洛的歌。"
哗哗的水声忽然消失，
桑洛的歌啊，钻进了娥并心里。

"猛根的河水呵！
你真是清凉，
甜得像甘蔗，
绿得像草地，
我想带几罐河水回家，
只怕没有福气。

"山上的瀑布啊！
你多么明亮，
就像一面大镜子，
对着太阳发光。

"河里的鲤鱼啊！
你躲藏在哪里？
我划过了每一个波浪，
就是为了把你找寻。

"猛根像一个天堂，
姑娘们像天上的仙女。
猛根雨后的草地，
爬满了金蚂蚁。
猛根美丽的姑娘，
比金蚂蚁还多。

"Oh, little river!
Please run lightly and quietly right now!
Let me hear Sangluo's singing!"
The river did suddenly become quiet,
and Sangluo's song flew directly into E'bing's heart.

"Oh, the river in Menggen!
How clear and how cool,
sweet like a sugarcane
and green like a lawn,
and I really would like to bring some water home with me,
but I am afraid I am not that lucky."

"Ah, waterfalls in the mountains!
How clean and how bright,
like giant mirrors
glisten under the sunshine."

"Ah, carps in the river!
Where are you hiding?
I row through every wave
just to look for you."

"Menggen is like a heavenly paradise,
full of beautiful fairies.
The lawns here after the rain
are full of golden ants.
But the beautiful young women in Menggen
outnumber the golden ants."

"磨得发光的宝石啊!
像象牙一样洁白,
是不是你吃的不是人间的米,
才会长得这样美丽?

"娥并的名字呵!
像鲜花的花粉,
被蜜蜂蝴蝶四处传去。
哥哥像一只蜜蜂,
从远方飞来采蜜。

"哥哥从景多昂来,
就是为了串妹妹,
为什么风吹荷花不摇摆?
为什么洗头的妹妹口不开?"

娥并听着桑洛的歌,
半句也没有放过。
她还怕听不清楚,
把散开的头发轻轻挽成一束。

"猛根的宝石呵!
你的光射到四面八方,
为什么心里的话,
却要搁在家里?
心里的歌应该带在身边。
随时都能唱出来。

"Ah, polished jewel!
You are as white as ivory.
Do you not eat the rice in this world
and is it why you are so beautiful?"

"Oh, the name of E'bing!
It is like the pollen of a fresh flower
that is spread by bees and butterflies.
I come like a bee, come especially for you from afar."

"I come from Jingduo'ang
just to get to know you.
Why doesn't the lotus flower sway in the breeze?
Why is the young sister washing her hair but not sing back?"

E'bing heard Sangluo's singing
and didn't miss anything.
To catch everything,
she tied up her hair into a bundle.

"Oh, the precious jewel of Menggen!
You shines everywhere,
but why did you leave your words of the heart at home?
Words of the heart should be brought along with you
so that you can sing them aloud anytime you want."

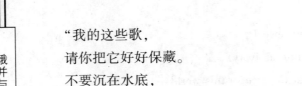

"我的这些歌，
请你把它好好保藏。
不要沉在水底，
不要被灰尘打脏。

"我唱的这些歌，
不要让它白白抛撒。
请你把它装进心里，
请你给景多昂的哥哥一句回答。"

桑洛的歌好听，
桑洛的歌就是他的爱情。
桑洛的爱情啊！
打动了娥并的心。

好像风吹树叶，
桑洛的心不住地跳。
娥并的歌像河里的流水，
逗得桑洛的心，
像小船一样在波浪上漂。

"捉鱼的哥哥呀！
你的歌声真好听，
你身上背着弩箭，
不是要去打野兽吗？
怎么又到河里来捉鱼？"

"My songs,
please take good care of them.
Don't let them sink to the riverbed
or be dirtied by the dust."

"My songs,
please do not let them be sung in vain.
Please keep them all in your heart
and please give me a word of response."

Sangluo's songs were pleasant,
the songs of love.
Ah, Sangluo's love!
It made E'bing so moved.

Like the leaves in the wind,
Sangluo's heart kept leaping.
E'bing's responsorial songs were like the flowing water,
making Sangluo's heart
feel like a boat floating with waves of the river.

"Ah, big brother the fisherman!
How pleasantly do you sing!
You carry a bow on your back,
so didn't you plan to go hunting?
How did you end up here fishing?"

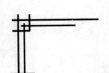
"你真像一个猎人，
手里却拿着渔网。
猎人应该到山林里去，
猎人怎么会坐在船上？

"在船上的哥哥呵！
为什么你的网只撒在水面？
是不是要叫鱼儿
自己跳进小船去？

"哥哥真会唱歌啊！
哥哥却一点不会捉鱼。
哥哥赶来了那么多黄牛，
哥哥是来做生意的。

"哥哥长得这样漂亮，
猛根没有姑娘配得上。
哥哥的歌是唱给娥并的，
这里没有一个姑娘叫娥并！"

"姑娘呀，
你像春天发芽的树叶，
又嫩又绿；
你像河边的金竹子，
又直又细。

"You look like a hunter,
yet you have a fishing net in your hands.
A hunter should be hunting in the forest,
but why are you on a boat?"

"Oh, big brother on the boat!
Why do you cast the net only onto the surface of the river?
Is it because you want the fish
to jump into the boat by themselves?"

"Ah, big brother, you are indeed a good singer!
But you don't know how to catch fish.
You had so many cattle with you,
and you are here to do business this time."

"Big brother! You are so handsome
that no young woman in Menggen is your match.
Your songs are for E'bing,
but there is no E'bing here."

"Oh, young lady!
You are like the spring sprouts,
tender and fresh;
you are like the golden bamboo,
graceful and slender."

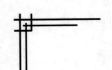
"你说这里没有娥并，
你却有娥并一样的眼睛，
有娥并一样的手臂，
有娥并一样的嘴唇！

"娥并的名字，
像粉团花一样芳香。
你说这里没有娥并，
我却闻到了粉团花的香味！

"不管这里有没有人叫娥并，
不管你的名字叫不叫娥并，
天神已经把我送到你的身边，
没有得到爱情啊，
我绝不回去！

"我离开了家乡，
赶着牛群到远方，
不是为了做生意，
是为了寻找心爱的姑娘。

"我到过无数的寨子，
我走过每一个山冈，
尝过山里的泉水，
尝过新鲜的茶叶，
没有一个地方，
像猛根这样美丽。

"You say there is no E'bing here,
but you have exactly the same eyes,
same arms
and same lips as her!"

"The name of E'bing!
It smells as pleasant as a hydrangea.
You say there is no E'bing here,
but I smell the hydrangea here."

"No matter whether there is any E'bing here,
or whether your name is E'bing,
Heaven has sent you to my side,
and without your love, I won't go back."

"I left my hometown
and herded cattle in so far a place,
not to do business,
but to find my love."

"I have been to numerous villages,
passed by every hill,
tasted the mountain spring water
and fresh tea,
but none of those places
is as beautiful as Menggen."

"我在家里，
时刻都想出门；
我在家里，
没有一天安静。
你好像一根绳子，
把远远的小船啊！
从景多昂拉到了猛根。"

听了桑洛的歌声，
娥并轻轻回答：
"花苞呀，一个一个挂在花树上；
鲜花呀，一朵一朵开在枝头上。
钓鱼的年轻小伙子啊，
你真会唱！
你的歌像芳香的板宝花，
香味吹在我的心上。

"我想摘下这朵花戴在胸前，
怕我的衣服配不上。
我怕自己长得太丑，
我怕旁人知道，
会乱说乱讲。"

"美丽的姑娘呀！
你好像一颗发光的钻石，
我在这里找到了它，
我永远要把它托在手里。

"When I was at home,
I always wanted to go out;
when I was at home,
I was always restless.
Ah, like a rope,
you pulled a small boat here from afar!
All the way from Jingduo'ang to Menggen."

On hearing Sangluo's songs,
E'bing replied in a soft voice:
"The fresh buds are hanging on the trees,
and the pretty flowers are blooming over the branches.
Ah, the young fisherman,
you are so good at singing
that your songs are like as sweet as Banbao flowers,
its fragrance touching my heart."

"I want to wear this Banbao flower① on my chest,
but I am afraid that my clothes are not gorgeous enough for it.
I worry that I am not good-looking enough for it,
and that others around
may gossip about me."

"Oh, beautiful young lady!
You are like a shining diamond,
which I have found
and which I will forever keep in my hands."

---

① Banbao flower is a local flower in the Dai area.

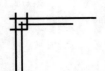

"我的爱情，
不像货物锁在箱子里，
我要唱出来，
让姑娘知道我的心意。

"姑娘呀！难道你的心，
你的爱情，
都是锁在家里，
没有带在身上吗？

"我的爱情啊！
无法隐藏，
我不讲就要唱，
不唱就要讲。

"猛根漂亮的姑娘这样多，
我爱的就是你一个。
你像高高山上的鲜花，
我穿过刺丛也要摘下。

"我离开景多昂，
离开了自己的家，
我像山巅上的鲜花，
自由自在地开放。

"My love

is not like a merchandise that is kept in a trunk,

so I must sing it out loud

and let you know my heart."

"Oh, young lady! Could it be that your heart

and your love

are locked at home,

not with you?"

"My love!

It is not hidden.

I must either sing

or speak about it."

"Of countless beautiful young women in Menggen,

I love only you.

You are like a beautiful fresh flower at the mountain peak,

and I must pick you regardless of thorny bushes along the

way."

"I left Jingduo'ang

and left my home.

I am like the fresh flowers at the top of mountains,

free to bloom."

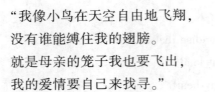
"我像小鸟在天空自由地飞翔，
没有谁能缚住我的翅膀。
就是母亲的笼子我也要飞出，
我的爱情要自己来找寻。"

"亲爱的哥哥呀！
如果你真喜欢这朵荷花，
你就要下水去采；
如果你真爱我，
我一定在家把你等待。"

"姑娘呀！
请把你的家告诉我，
等到太阳偏西，
我一定会来串你。

"如果不能和你在一起，
一辈子没有幸福！
如果不能同建一座塔，
死也不甘心！"

"我家住在街头上，
来往的人都要经过，
做生意的人爱在门外谈笑，
小孩子们爱在门边玩耍。

"I am like a little birds in the sky,
no one can stop me from spreading my wings.
Even my mother's cage
I must escape to look for my love by myself."

"Oh, dear big brother!
If you really like a lotus flower,
you must get into the water to pick it!
If you really love me,
I will await you at my home."

"Oh, young lady!
Please tell me where you live.
At sunset,
I will be sure to visit you at your home."

"If I cannot be with you,
I won't have happiness in my life!
If I can't build the same tower with you①,
it will be the biggest regret in my life!"

"Our house is at the end of the main street,
where everyone passes by,
where businessmen like to gather together, laughing and
talking,
and where kids like to play."

---

① In the Dai's custom, good couples usually save money together to build a tower of Buddhism in order to pray for being together in next life.

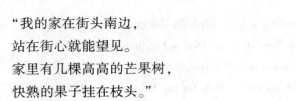

"我的家在街头南边，
站在街心就能望见。
家里有几棵高高的芒果树，
快熟的果子挂在枝头。"

桑洛听见连连答应，
小船在岸边靠拢，
娥并也准备回家，
把洗好的衣服放进水桶。

"Our house is on the south side at the end of the main
street,

which can be seen from the center of the main street.

We have several tall mango trees in our yard

with many almost ripened mangoes on them."

Sangluo agreed repeatedly

and steered his boat to the riverbank,

and E'bing was also ready to go home,

putting the cleaned-up clothes into water buckets.

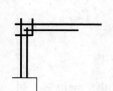
八

桑洛的歌啊，
像丁香花正在开放；
日子愈长，
开得愈浓郁。

桑洛回到住处，
只望太阳快落山，
娥并回到家，
只望月亮快升起。

她早早就坐着纺线，
纺车转得特别响，
线也纺得特别多，
装满了一个个小竹箩。

8

Ah , Sangluo's songs!
They were like blooming lilacs :
the longer they bloom ,
the more fragrant they become.

When Sangluo went back ,
all he waited for was the sunset.
When E'bing went home ,
all she longed for was the moonrise①.

She started early and sat in front of the spinning wheel to
spin the yarn② ,
　　with the wheel running quite loudly
　　and the thread were in large amount ,
　　with the baskets filled one after another.

---

①　It's one of Dai's tradition that young men go to visit their beloved at
their houses at night , waiting outside , playing the qin or whistling the flute ,
until the young women go out of their house by themselves.

②　It's another custom for a young woman to sit weavings in front of
her house , hiding an extra stool under her dress especially for the young men
she sees in.

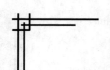

娥并与桑洛 E'bing and Sangluo

爱情啊！像天上的月亮，
怎么还不升起？
走夜路的人，
正等着你的光芒。

太阳落山了，
桑洛背上了琴，
走到猛根街子上。
找到了娥并的家。

他轻轻弹着琴，
娥并早已听得仔细。
这不是猛根小伙子弹的，
这琴弹得多好听！

娥并停下了纺车，
拿起了口弦，
桑洛已经走到楼下，
来到她的身边。

娥并的母亲看见桑洛，
心里再不为女儿焦急。
她叫女儿快快打扫竹楼，
把远方的客人请上楼去。

102

Ah, Love! Why would you be like the moon
taking your time to rise tonight?
Those walking at night
were still awaiting your light.

Finally, the sun had set.
Sangluo carried his qin on his back,
went along the street in Menggen,
and found E'bing's home.

He played the qin gently,
and E'bing listened carefully.
She knew this couldn't be played by any young man in
Menggen,
and how tuneful it was!

She stopped the spinning wheel
and took out her Kouxianqin.
And Sangluo had already arrived downstairs
and come by her side.

At sight of Sangluo,
E'bing's mother was not worried for her daughter anymore.
She asked E'bing to hurry and clean the bamboo hut
and to let in Sangluo, the guest from afar.

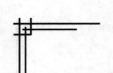

娥并在火塘边铺好一床褥子：
"哥哥请褥子上坐！
只怕我家竹楼不平，
真对不起哥哥。"

娥并拿出水罐，
给桑洛倒了一碗水：
"哥哥请喝水吧！
只怕我们家的水不甜。"

娥并捧着草烟和槟榔，
亲手递给桑洛：
"太阳落坡的时候，
我就为哥哥准备好了。"

"你家的褥子，
比我家的床还平软；
你家的凉水，
比我家的糖还甜。"

E'bing put up a mattress① by the fireplace:
"Please take a seat, big brother!
I am afraid the floor of our hut is not leveled enough
and wish we had something better to offer you."

She got out a water pot
and poured him a bowl of water:
"Dear Sangluo, please have some water!
I'm afraid that our water here is not sweet enough."

She held areca nuts and tobacco②,
and presented them to him herself:
"By the time of sunset,
I had finished preparing them especially for you."

"The cushion at your house
is softer than the one I have at home,
and the water here
is sweeter than the candy in my hometown."

---

① In the Dai families, the mattresses are usually put on the ground for their guests to sit on as a cushion.

② It's quite common for the Dai people to entertain the guests by arecas nuts and tobaccos.

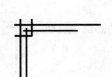
琴声停止了，
口弦弹响了：
"天神送到猛根来的哥哥呀！
凉水好喝你可以挖一条沟，
让它流到景多昂去。
猛根的花好戴呵，
你可以连根挖走，
用泉水把鲜花浇养。

"只怕我笨手织的粗布，
配不上哥哥的细绸缎；
只怕我采的野菜和番茄，
让哥哥吃饭时难下咽。"

"水银般的妹妹呀！
猛根的好姑娘！
桑洛各地都挑遍，
再细的绸料子，
也比不上猛根的粗布；
再苦的果子，
在猛根也会变甜。

"只怕哥哥和妹妹相隔太远，
见一次面要走三十天；
只怕妹妹是镜子里的花，
我看得见却挨不到身边。
像水里的月亮，
哥哥一伸手浪花就把月光隐藏。"

106

Sangluo stopped playing the qin,
and E'bing began to play the Kouxianqin：
"Oh, big brother from Menggen sent by Heaven!
If you like the water here, you can dig a ditch,
along which the water will flow to Jingduo'ang.
If you like the flowers here,
you can transplant them
and nourish them by using the spring water."

"I'm afraid that the cloth I weaved clumsily
is not refined enough to match the elegant silk you wear,
and that the wild vegetables and tomatoes I picked
are not appetizing enough for your taste."

"Oh, my mercury-like E'bing!
A nice young lady of Menggen!
I have been to various places
and found that silkiest of the materials
is still inferior to the rough cloth in Menggen,
and the bitterest fruits in Menggen
turn out to be sweet."

"I am afraid that we are too far apart,
so it takes thirty days of journey for us to see each other.
I am afraid that you are like the image of a flower in the mirror,
visible yet untouchable,
or the image of the moon in the pond,
hiding behind the waves every time I reach to touch it."

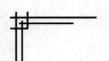
"远方的哥哥呀!
世间这样宽广,
再远的路我们也能走完。
只要心里相爱,
三百天相见一次也情愿。

"我像悬岩上的野果,
没有人来采过;
我像岩石下的花苞,
没有虫子爬过。

"我们地方的姑娘,
一句话比金子珍贵。
只要哥哥不变心,
我们的爱情呵,
没有人能够拆散!"

"猛根的花呀!
我摘下了你,
别人用鲜花我也不换,
我走过深山老林,
不让你淋着雨,
不让你在路上枯萎,
我的心啊!
要像泥土和泉水,
细细地把你栽培。"

"Oh, big brother from afar!
The world is big indeed,
but we will make it in distance no matter how big it is.
With the love between us,
we are willing to try even if we can only see each other once
in every three hundred days."

"I am like a wild berry on the cliff
that no one touched before;
I am like a bud under the rock
that no bug crawled over before."

"We young women of Menggen,
our words are more precious than gold.
As long as you do not change your mind,
our love will never be hurt by anyone!"

"Oh, the flower of Menggen!
I have picked you
and won't exchange with others no matter how fresh they are.
Crossing remote montains and forests,
I will shelter you from the strong rain
and keep you from the scorching sun.
Ah, my heart!
It is like the soil and the spring water,
cherishing you, cultivating you and nourishing you."

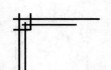

这时，火光映着娥并的耳环，
一闪一闪，
两人都沉默无言，
爱情已深深埋进他们心间。
爱情啊！
像粉团花一样发出芳香，
两对眼睛都为爱情发光。
爱情啊！
不怕风吹雨打，
已像扭在一起的藤子，
没有什么能拆散。

说不完的话，
表白不尽的情意，
两人的情话要是写成书，
三个奘房也装不完；
好像一个深深的井水，
舀不尽，打不干。

月亮已经西沉，
天上只剩下最后一颗星星。
火塘的火渐渐熄灭了，
天快亮了。

太阳升起来了，
驱散山野里的浓雾。
母亲听见了桑洛的一片真情，
她暗暗地为女儿祝福。

At this moment, with E'bing's earrings glistening
with the reflection of the firelight,
they fell into silence
and were deeply connected by their love for each other.
Ah, love!
Like a hydrangea releasing its fragrance,
their eyes radiated with the light of love.
Ah, love!
Like the entangled vines,
regardless of no matter the wind or the rain,
they become inseparable.

Words they had for each other were endless,
and feelings they felt for each other were boundless.
If written into books,
there would be so many of them
that three Zangfangs would not be enough to hold them;
like the water of a deep well,
those words and feelings were inexhaustible.

The moon set to the west,
with only the last star left twinkling.
The fire in the fireplace went out,
and the day was almost breaking.

The sun rose,
and soon the thick fog fade into wilderness.
E'bing's mother heard the love uttered by Sangluo
and wished silently for her daughter's happiness.

三天过去了，
七天八天过去了，
二十个傍晚也在爱情中消磨。
每天天快亮，
桑洛才回到住的地方。

朋友们早已知道，
大家议论纷纷，
谈着桑洛的事情。
有的跟他开玩笑，
有的好心为他祝贺，
有的说他真是幸运，
到远方找到了心爱的人。
有的为桑洛担心，
怕他的母亲知道，
会阻拦他们的爱情……

小伙子们出门太久，
货物早已卖完。
买来的东西，
又把牛驮子装满。

朋友们不停地劝说，
桑洛不能不听。
动身前的夜晚，
桑洛来向娥并告别：

Three days had passed,
then a week,
and twenty days of loving had passed.
Every day Sangluo returned to his place
but not before the dawn.

All his friends knew
and began to talked,
Some joking with Sangluo,
some congratulating him,
some thinking he was lucky to find his true love from afar,
while some worrying about him
for fear that his mother would stop their love①...

The group of young men had stayed out for quite a long time,
and now everything had been sold out.
They loaded up the cattle
with the newly purchased staff.

Sangluo couldn't ignore
what his friends kept telling him.
The night before they set off for home,
he came to say goodbye to E'bing:

---

① The marriage between two people from different social ranks in the
Dai will not be blessed and usually be prevented by older generations.

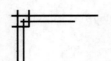

"正开放的荷花呀！
我要回家乡去了。
我们共同栽的花，
不要让旁人摘下；
我们一起引来的泉水，
不要让旁人来汲取。

"漂亮的鲜花啊，
离开你，哥哥心里多么难过！
亲爱的姑娘，
把我俩的爱情包起来，
紧紧地锁在箱子里吧，
不要让别人抢去。

"我回家要告诉母亲，
准备好礼物骑上马再来娶你。
亲爱的娥并啊！
牢牢记住我的话吧，
我请求你送我一朵花，
让它伴着我回去。"

"Oh, blooming lotus flower!
I have to go home tomorrow.
The flower we cultivated together,
do not let it be picked by others;
the spring water we channeled here,
do not let it be used by others!"

"Ah, pretty blossom!
I'm so sad to leave you like this!
Dear young lady,
please pack up our love
and lock it up in a box
so that no one can steal it!"

"I'll tell my mother everything
and bring the marriage gifts next time I come to marry you①.
Ah, dear E'bing!
do remember my words,
and please give me a flower
and let it accompany me back."

---

①　When a young man and a young woman fall in love, it's usually the young man's family that invites all the family relatives to a formal dinner to inform everyone of their engagement.

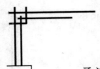
桑洛要回景多昂，
娥并心里多焦急：
"桑洛哥哥呀！
你要回到景多昂去。
家乡的姑娘，
又会在路边迎接你；
牛群的铃声，
会使家乡的人欢喜。

"亲爱的哥哥呀！
骑上你喜爱的马，
慢慢地回家去吧。
你什么时候离开猛根，
我的心也跟你去到景多昂。

"我俩的爱情永远不会改变，
就是天上的仙人
来和我谈情，
我也不愿意。

"桑洛哥哥啊！
记住我俩的爱情吧！
到了你的家乡，
不要把我遗忘。"

Sangluo was leaving for Jingduo'ang,
and E'bing was anxious and upset:
"Oh, big brother Sangluo!
You are leaving for Jingduo'ang.
The girls in your hometown
will greet you along the roadsides
and the bell ringing of cattle
will please everyone there."

"Oh, big brother Sangluo!
Ride your favorite horse
and take your time to return to your hometown.
The time you leave Menggen
is the time my heart starts to follow you to Jingduo'ang."

"Our love will never change,
and even if a god comes,
he will not
win me over."

"Ah, big brother Sangluo!
Remember our love!
On returning to your hometown,
don't forget me."

117

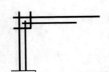

娥并与桑洛　E'bing and Sangluo

天快亮了，
红公鸡伸着脖子叫，
桑洛就要离开娥并了。
他俩的心啊，
像一朵鲜花，
被摘下来丢在路上一样了。

天刚刚发亮，
猛根的姑娘都起了床。
不是去挑水，
不是去摘菜，
是听见了牛铃声，
去给桑洛送行。

有的站在园子边，
有的站在大青树下，
有的躲在篱笆后面，
有的伏在栏杆上，
看着桑洛走过去。

桑洛的朋友们，
取下了牛脖子上的铃铛。
桑洛的心，
闷得说不出一句话，
唱不出一句歌。

118

It was at dawn,

with roosters crowing outside,

that Sangluo was about to leave E'bing.

Ah, both of their hearts,

they felt like a fresh flower

picked but abandoned by the roadside.

At daybreak,

all the young women in Menggen had got up,

but not for carrying water,

nor for picking vegetables,

but, on hearing the bell ringing of cattle,

for seeing off Sangluo.

Some stood next to yards,

some stood under great green trees,

some hid behind bamboo fences

and some leaned against rails,

all watching Sangluo passing by.

Sangluo's friends

untied the bells from cattle,

and Sangluo

felt so sad that he could not say any word

or sing any note.

娥并站在篱笆后面，
偷偷地哭泣！
她说不出话，
眼泪一滴一滴滚下来。

桑洛走远了，
影子看不见了，
娥并忍不住哭出声来。
又怕别人知道，
用裙子捂住嘴，
泪水已把衣裙湿透。

E'bing stood behind a bamboo fence,
weeping!
She could not speak at all,
but her tears rolled down one after another.

When Sangluo walked far away
and then his silhouette vanished.
E'bing couldn't help crying.
Not wanting others to know,
she had to cover her mouth with her skirt,
soaking her skirt all with tears.

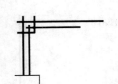

九

一队牛群往回走，
没有铃声也没有人声。
牛头上绿茵茵的孔雀毛，
像大雨前的森林。

路啊，弯弯扭扭，
像在鸡冠上一样难走。
森林里一片烟雾，
雀鸟也不愿飞出窝。

桑洛回到家里，
亲戚朋友都来欢迎，
有的来问外地的风光，
有的来尝点春茶和槟榔。

家里挤满了客人，
大家都有说有笑，
只有桑洛，
满脸的愁苦，
一句话也不说。

9

The herd of cattle was proceeding quietly,
without bell ringing or men's talking.
The green peacock tail feathers on the cattle's heads
looked like a forest before a heavy rain.

The winding road
was as rugged as the edge of cockscombs to walk on,
and the forest fog
was too dense for birds to leave their nests.

When Sangluo arrived at home,
his relatives and friends all came to welcome him,
some curious about the sceneries out there
and others wanting to taste the spring tea and the areca nuts.

His home was full of guests
talking and laughing,
but Sangluo
looked sorrowful
and spoke not any word.

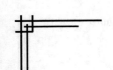
桑洛回到家呵，
琴弦再也不响，
他只想着娥并，
只想偷偷去到猛根。

"山啊！
你为什么这样高？
低下来吧，
让我看看猛根在哪里！

"云啊！
飘到猛根去吧！
去看看我的娥并，
是不是在悲伤流泪？"

桑洛整天忧伤，
什么话也不愿讲。
母亲问他是生了病，
还是做生意亏了本？
桑洛没有回答。

母亲去向他的朋友探问，
朋友们说出了真情。
桑洛的母亲知道了儿子的心事，
准备把儿子狠狠教训。

Sangluo was home,
but he no longer played the qin.
He only missed E'bing
and wanted to sneak out to Menggen.

"Ah, mountains!
Why are you so high?
Please bow your head
and let me see where Menggen is!"

"Ah, clouds!
Please float to Menggen
to take a look at my E'bing!
Is she sad and weeping?"

Distressed all day long,
Sangluo did not feel like talking.
His mother asked him if he was not well
or lost money with the business.
But he said nothing.

When she asked his friends,
they told her everything.
Knowing now what was troubling her son,
she was ready to scold him severely.

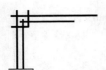

桑洛天天想念娥并，
他不理睬母亲的反复盘问。
这天趁母亲熟睡，
他又骑上马去到猛根。

桑洛在猛根住了很久，
日子一天天过去；
娥并的脸渐渐消瘦，
她已经怀孕了。

娥并看见自己和以前不同，
她告诉桑洛：
"你不要在猛根住得太长了，
我已经怀孕了。
你快快离开猛根吧，
告诉母亲再来接我。"

"亲爱的娥并啊！
你不要发愁，
不过一个月，
我一定来接你。
我去了很快就来，
你等着我吧。"

Sangluo kept missing E'bing every single day,
and he ignored his mother's repeated questioning.
One day when his mother was sleeping,
he sneaked out and rode horse towards Menggen.

Sangluo lived in Menggen for quite a long time,
one day and then another days.
E'bing became thinner
because she was now pregnant.

Seeing how different she looked from before,
E'bing told Sangluo:
"Please don't stay here for too long,
for I am pregnant.
Leave Menggen quickly
to tell your mother and then come to get me soon.①"

"Ah, dear E'bing!
Don't worry,
within a month,
I will come to get you.
I will be back soon.
Please wait for me."

---

① There are many taboos for pregnant women in the Dai culture, for both mothers and babies are considered vulnerable to evil things. For example. they are not allowed to walk out frequently nor touch any men's weapons or production tools, which will bring bad luck to them and their family members.

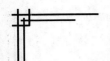

桑洛回到家，
立刻把事情告诉了母亲。
母亲听完就变了脸，
拉开嗓子大骂：

"不知羞耻的畜生，
我用一滴滴水、一口口饭，
白白把你喂养成人，
偏偏你要跑到外乡，
干出这种丑事情！

"我只想，
你出门会找回金银；
想不到，
你会和猛根的姑娘谈情！
亲戚家的好姑娘你不要，
偏偏去找魔鬼样的女人！

"你在我的家里，
就得听我管教，
要是再不规矩，
从此不要叫我母亲！"

As soon as Sangluo returned home,

he told his mother everything.

On learning about what had happened,

his mother burst into a fit of anger, yelling:

"You shameless beast,

I was the one who brought you up with one drop of water at a time

and one mouth of rice at a time,

but you rewarded me with such shameful behaviors

in such a faraway place!①"

"I thought

you would bring back gold and silver.

Never did it occur to me

that you would dare to date some young woman in Menggen!

Fine young women among your relatives you refused,

but ghastly ones from afar you chose."

"As long as you stay in my house,

you must do what I say.

If you don't behave yourself,

don't call me your mother anymore."

---

①　The marriages in ancient Dai were usually arranged according to religious beliefs, vested interests and other aspects of two people, such as lineage, social ranks and wealth, so the Dai people seldom married those from other ethnic minority groups or other ranks.

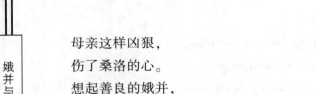

母亲这样凶狠，
伤了桑洛的心。
想起善良的娥并，
桑洛再也不能容忍：

"老年人怎懂得年轻人的心？
年轻人怎能违背自己的爱情？
母亲的话我都听，
这件事绝不能答应！

"娥并是最好的姑娘，
娥并是最好的妻子！
我偏偏要和她成亲！
如果你真不答应，
从此我不叫你母亲！"

桑洛这些话，
气白了母亲的嘴唇，
她知道儿子的脾气，
又用软言来劝引：

"妈妈的桑洛呀！
你要听母亲的话：
外地的姑娘
不会使你快活，
外地的姑娘又丑又笨！

Sangluo was saddened
by his mother's fierceness and cruelty.
Thinking of E'bing,
he couldn't bear it any more.

"How could the old know the hearts of the young?
How could the young betray their love?
I can do anything else you ask of me,
but cannot obey you on this matter."

"E'bing is the best young lady
and the best wife!
I must marry her!
If you won't give us your blessing,
I will not call you mother from now on."

These words by Sangluo
were so upsetting to his mother that her lips turned white
with anger,
but she knew her son,
so she turned to softer words:

"Oh, my Sangluo!
Please do what I say:
the girls elsewhere
won't make you happy
and they are all ugly and clumsy!"

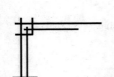

"她们织的一块布呀，
不够做一件衣服；
她们织的布，
像牛脖子一样粗。

"桑洛呀！
你出去这样久，
阿扁还是爱着你。
她聪明得像小鸟，
她织的布呀，
又结实又有花纹。

"你是景多昂沙铁的儿子，
怎么会爱上猛根的穷姑娘？
她们织的布，
作头巾也不够，
作手绢也不配。

"她们笨手笨脚，
织的丝绸呀，
看起来黑漆漆，
穿起来冷冰冰。

"远方的姑娘，
只会爱你一时，
你要有了疾病，
她们就会把你抛弃。"

"Each piece of cloth they weave
is not enough to make a shirt.
The cloth they weave
is as rough as the skin of cattle's neck."

"Oh, Sangluo!
You have been gone for such a long time,
but A'bian still loves you.
She is as smart as a little bird,
and the cloth she weaves is sturdy with refined patterns."

"You are the son of a Shatie in Jingduo'ang,
but how could you fall in love with a poor young woman from
Menggen?
The cloth they weave
is not big enough even for a headscarf,
nor good enough even for a handkerchief."

"They are so clumsy
that the silk they weave
looks dark
and is cold to touch!"

"The young women from afar
will love you only for a while,
and when you are sick
they will abandon you."

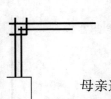

母亲这些话，
儿子不愿听，
桑洛一心挂念着娥并，
邻居和朋友也为他伤心。

Those words from his mother
were what the son did not want to listen to,
with Sangluo keeping thinking only of E'bing all the time,
his neighbors and friends felt so sorry for him.

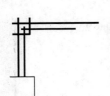

十

年轻的姑娘和小伙子们，
他俩的痛苦多么深！
好好地听吧，
我要让我的歌，
打动人们的心！

桑洛离开猛根，
娥并日夜等待，
左也不见来，
右也不见来，
腰身一天天地大了。
可怜的娥并呵！
日日盼望着，
夜夜在哭泣！

"桑洛哥哥呀！
你怎么到今天还不来？
当初我像荷花开放，
你每日每夜在我身旁；
是不是荷花枯萎了，
哥哥再不愿走近池塘？

10

Young men and young women,
how deep is their pain!
Please listen carefully,
and I'll let my song
move everyone!

After Sangluo left Menggen,
E'bing waited day and night,
and she waited, and waited,
but did not see him return,
only her waist becoming bigger and bigger.
Oh, poor E'bing!
She expected every day
and cried every night.

"Oh, big brother Sangluo!
Why haven't you come back yet?
I used to be like a blossoming lotus flower
with you by my side day and night;
is it because the flower is withering
and you don't want to approach the pond anymore?"

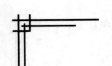

"桑洛呀!
你像森林里的鹿,
不想再看见猎人!
怎么还不回到猛根?
娥并不是森林里的猎人。

"亲爱的桑洛呀!
我多么害羞呀,
没有什么痛苦能和我相比。
回到你的家想不起我了吧,
怎么还不来接我啊!
如果我知道
你要离开这样久,
我一定跟着你去了!

"桑洛呀!
我俩的爱情,
像结在一起的丝线那样紧。
为什么到今天,
还不见你的身影?"

痛苦啊,
像千斤重担,
压在娥并双肩!
母亲知道了也为女儿焦急:

"Oh, Sangluo!
You are like a deer in a forest
that doesn't want to meet hunters!
Is that why you haven't returned to Menggen?
But E'bing is not a hunter."

"Oh, dear Sangluo!
So embarrassed I am
that no pain could be compared with mine!
Have you forgotten about me once you returned home,
or else why you are not coming to get me?
If I knew
you would leave me for this long,
I would have definitely gone with you!"

"Oh, Sangluo!
Our love
is as tight as silk threads.
Why up to now
haven't you shown up yet?"

Ah, the pain,
like a thousand-kilo burden,
weighed on E'bing's shoulders!
Her mother became worried for her:

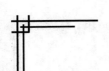

"亲爱的女儿啊！
你已经长大成人，
你的事情由你决定，
我们不阻挡你，
快去找桑洛吧！"

娥并收拾了几件衣衫，
匆匆离开了猛根。
她第一次走这样远啊，
三个姑娘陪着她一起出门。

走过无数个寨子，
渡过无数条大江，
爬过无数座高山，
路啊，还是那么遥远。

路上没有桑洛的脚印，
林中不见桑洛的牛群。
粉团花一样的娥并呀！
她去问放牛的青年：

"放牛的哥哥们！
你们在这里放牛，
有没有看见桑洛？
到景多昂走哪一条路？"

"Ah, my dear daughter!
You are already an adult,
so it's up to you to decide your affairs.
We won't stop you
if you want to go and look for Sangluo!"

E'bing packed a few pieces of clothing,
and left Menggen in a haste.
It was the first time she had gone this far,
so three young women accompanied her.

They passed countless villages,
crossed numerous rivers
and climbed many mountains,
but the journey was rather a long one.

There were no Sangluo's footprints on the way
or Sangluo's cattle in the forest,
so hydrangea-like E'bing
went to ask some herds boys:

"Big brothers, cattle herders!
Since you have been herding cattle here,
did you see Sangluo?
Which road can take us to Jingduo'ang?"

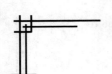

"姑娘呵！
你仔细记住：
前面的路有几条，
到景多昂的路最难走。
你要走向日出的东方，
那就能找到桑洛。"

不知走了多少天，
走过了密密的森林，
走过了大石桥，
看见了河边高高的金塔，
娥并来到了景多昂的寨头。

四个姑娘在河里洗了澡，
娥并换上新衣服，
抖了抖裙子，
戴上了鲜花和金手镯。

跟娥并来的姑娘，
头发也梳得很亮，
她们走进了寨子，
寻找桑洛住的地方。

桑洛的母亲，
早就猜到娥并要来，
心里的主意啊，
比魔鬼还要毒。

"Oh, young ladies!
Listen carefully and be prepared:
among several roads in front of you,
the one to Jingduo'ang is roughest.
Keep going eastward towards the sunrise,
and you will find Sangluo."

They did not know how many more days they continued,
walking through dense forests
and crossing big stone bridges,
but when they saw a golden tower high up by the river,
they knew they had arrived at the gate of Jingduo'ang.

The four young women bathed in the river,
E'bing changed a new blouse,
shook her skirt
and put on some fresh flowers and gold bracelets.

The young women who accompanied E'bing
also dressed their hair nice and shiny,
and they went into the village
and began to look for Sangluo's house.

Sangluo's mother
expected E'bing to make a trip here,
so she made up a plan
that was more vicious than a devil itself.

她收藏了家里的金银，
锁上了家里的箱柜，
用甜言蜜语对桑洛说：
"这几天你这样着急，
是不是娥并要来？
她来了我要请客，
家里却还没有酒菜。

"你快到河边去吧，
去打点鱼回来。
家里有我照顾，
她到了我替你招待。"

母亲的甜言蜜语，
儿子信以为真。
桑洛刚刚出去，
母亲就关上房门。

她找来许多竹片，
削得像针一样尖，
把竹针插在楼梯上，
插在竹墙上，
插在门上。
在装饭的盒子里，
藏起一把锋利的刀。

She put the gold and silver away,
locked up all the cabinets,
and asked Sangluo nicely:
"You seem so anxious these days.
Could it be that E'bing is coming?
If so, I would like to entertain her as a guest,
but we have nothing to go with the drink at home."

"Hurry and go to the river
to catch some fishes.
I will take care of everything here
and care for her, too, on behalf of you when she comes."

Mother's sweet talk
the son believed,
but as soon as Sangluo left,
his mother locked the door.

She found many bamboo chips,
sharpened them so that they were like needles,
and inserted them into bamboo stairs,
bamboo walls
and bamboo doors.
She then hid a sharp knife
in the rice bucket.

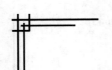

娥并走进了寨子，
心想着姑姑嫂嫂会来接她，
姐姐妹妹会来牵着她的手，
桑洛会来帮她背上包裹。

可是，没有一个人来接她，
也没有人和她打招呼。
三个姑娘陪着她，
进了桑洛的家。
家里不见桑洛的影子，
只有桑洛的母亲。
娥并恭恭敬敬对她行礼，
好言好语对她说话。

桑洛的母亲，
一句话不说，
脸酸溜溜的，
弯得像犁耙。

她一见娥并，
鼻子就翘起来。
弯弯扭扭的心啊，
像狗尾巴一样摇摆。

她去端来饭菜，
放在娥并面前。
她的脸酸得像木瓜，
她的声音装得像蜜糖：

E'bing walked into the village,
expecting that aunts would greet her,
sisters would hold her hands,
and Sangluo would help her carry her bags.

But no one came to meet her
and no one greeted her.
The three young women accompanied her
to enter Sangluo's home,
where she found no Sangluo
but only his mother.
E'bing bowed to her respectfully
and greeted her kindly.

Sangluo's mother
said nothing,
with a sour face
as bent as a plough.

At sight of E'bing,
she held up her nose
and her crooked mind
was wagging like a dog's tail.

She fetched some dishes
and put them in front of E'bing.
Her face was unpleasant like a papaya,
but she faked a voice as sweet as honey.

"桑洛怎么还不回来，
是不是碰见了老虎？
你不要为他着急，
先吃点饭再等他吧！

"腌菜是昨天才腌的，
你们来了正好碰上；
这些鱼啊，
都是桑洛为你预备的。"

桌上的东西，
哪里像人吃的！
帕贡菜像药一样苦，
腌鱼又生又臭。

娥并心里难过，
一口也咽不下。
看看母亲就要发怒，
她只好去添饭。
娥并不知道，
饭盒里会有尖刀；
娥并不知道，
母亲会有魔鬼的心肠。

"Why hasn't Sangluo come back yet?
Did he encounter a tiger?
But you don't need to worry about him,
and eat something while you wait for him!"

"The pickles were made yesterday,
so you are lucky enough to taste it now;
and these fishes
Sangluo prepared especially for you."

The dishes on the table
were actually not edible.
The Pagong dish① was as bitter as medicines,
and the pickled fishes were raw and smelly.

E'bing was so sad
that she couldn't swallow anything at all.
Seeing that his mother was about to burst into anger,
E'bing went to get another bowl of rice,
without knowing the sharp knife hidden in the rice bucket;
and without knowing
that his mother's heart was as vicious as that of a devil.

---

①　The Pagong dish is a famous Dai dish with local wild vegetables.

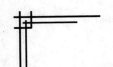
娥并去抓饭，
刀割破了她的手指，
娥并痛得昏了过去。
她急忙去开门，
门上的竹针又刺进了手心；
她靠在竹墙上，
墙上的竹针又刺进了背。

鲜红的血啊，
浸透了娥并的衣服。
三个姑娘看见，
连忙把她扶住，

娥并伤心哭，
呼唤着桑洛，
可是桑洛还在河边打鱼，
她眼前都是陌生的人。

眼泪一滴一滴落下来，
血一滴一滴掉下来。
血一直滴到楼下，
滴在楼下白公鸡身上，
把白公鸡都染红了；
滴在红公鸡身上，
把红公鸡都染成紫色。

When E'bing reached for the pilaf① in the rice bucket,

the knife cut her fingers

and she passed out from the pain;

when she later reached for the door,

her palm was pierced by the bamboo thorns on it;

when she leaned against the wall,

she was stabbed on the back by the bamboo nails on the

wall.

Ah, the scarlet blood

soaked her blouse.

At sight of this,

the three young women rushed to hold her by her sides.

E'bing sobbed sadly,

kept calling for Sangluo

who was still fishing by the river,

and in front of her were but strangers.

Tears rolled down drop by drop,

and blood ran downstairs drip by drip.

When it dropped on the white roosters downstairs,

it dyed them red;

When it dropped on the red ones,

it dyed them purple.

---

① In ancient Dai, rice, also called pilaf, is held in the rice bucket
and eaten with hands.

151

桑洛的母亲指着大门，
高声骂娥并：
"我家的饭菜不好吃，
你就放下碗筷！
我家的屋子不好住，
你就快些离开！
我的儿子桑洛，
娶不上你这个媳妇。"

Sangluo's mother pointed at the door,

yelling at E'bing:

"If the dishes in my house are not tasty to you,

you can put down the bowls and chopsticks!

If the rooms in my house are not comfortable for you,

you can leave now.

My son, Sangluo,

cannot marry you as his wife."

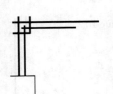

十一

娥并被赶出来了，
像牲口被主人赶出门。
猛根的姑娘啊！
她只能站在门外啼哭，
呼唤桑洛哥哥：

"我的桑洛呀！
你现在在哪儿？
你的娥并刚到你家，
就被你母亲赶出来了。

"我身上流着血，
你快快来吧。
你怎么还不来啊？
为什么还不见你的影子？"

一边走，一边哭，
美丽的娥并，
哭哑了嗓子。
头发散下来了，
头巾落下来了，
耳环掉在地上，
血从手上滴到地上。

11

E'bing was kicked out of the house,
like a cattle abandoned by its owner.
Ah, E'bing of Menggen!
She could but stand there sobbing,
calling for Sangluo:

"Oh, my Sangluo!
Where on earth are you now?
As soon your E'bing arrived at your house,
she was kicked out by your mother."

"I'm bleeding now.
Please come soon.
Why haven't you come?
Why haven't you shown up?"

Walking and sobbing,
beautiful E'bing's voice became hoarse,
her hair loosened,
her scarf dropped,
her earrings fell to the ground,
and her hands bleeding to the ground.

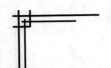
身边的三个姑娘，
一路上拾着掉下的东西；
她们跟着娥并哭，
一面哭，一面往后看：

"桑洛呀桑洛！
你的妻子从猛根来，
你的妻子遭到伤害，
你怎么不快快来看一眼！
这样生疏的地方，
我们到哪里去找你?"

三个姑娘扶着娥并，
走进一片树林，
娥并走不动了，
衣裙浸透了鲜血。

娥并呼唤着桑洛：
"刚开的攀枝花呀，
被风一吹，
花瓣纷纷散落；
刚离家的娥并呀，
遇见老虎，
快死在森林里了。

"我不愿死啊，
我不愿离开桑洛哥哥。
我的儿子还没有出世，
儿子还没有看见父亲。"

The three young women
were picking up the dropped items,
crying with her
and kept looking back:

"Sangluo, oh Sangluo!
Your wife came from Menggen,
and was mistreated.
Why don't you come to take a look at her!
This is such a unfamiliar place,
and where can we look for you?"

The three young women helped E'bing
to walk into a forest,
but E'bing couldn't move any further,
her blouse and skirt soaked in blood.

She kept calling for Sangluo:
"Oh, silk cotton flowers that just bloomed !
They are scattering pedals everywhere in the wind.
Oh, E'bing who just left her home,
she is dying in the forest,
having been attacked by a tiger."

"I don't want to die,
and I don't want to leave you big brother Sangluo.
My son isn't yet born,
nor has he seen his father."

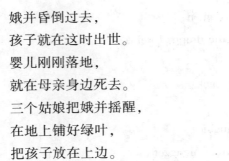

娥并昏倒过去，
孩子就在这时出世。
婴儿刚刚落地，
就在母亲身边死去。
三个姑娘把娥并摇醒，
在地上铺好绿叶，
把孩子放在上边。

"可怜的孩子啊！
你才出生就死去了。
没有尝到母亲一口奶，
没有得到父亲的疼爱。

"刚生下的孩子啊！
我怎舍得用泥土掩埋？
放在河里鱼要吃，
放在地上蚂蚁要搬，
放在池塘里青蛙要咬，
只好把你放在树上，
用树叶轻轻覆盖。

"亲爱的孩子呵！
你死在森林里，
灵魂不要跑到远方。

E'bing passed out,

and the child was born at that moment.

The moment he was born,

he died instantly by his mother's side.

The three young women woke up E'bing,

covered an area with green leaves,

and laid the child on them.

"Ah, poor child!

You died the moment you were born.

You didn't taste a drop of your mother's milk

nor enjoy an ounce of your father's love."

"Ah, poor child who was just born!

How could I bury you in soil like this?

But in the river you will be eaten by fish,

on the ground you will be moved by ants,

and in the pond you will be bitten by frogs.

I can only put you up in a tree and cover you gently with

leaves.①"

"Oh, my dear child!

You died in the forest,

and your spirit doesn't run to faraway places.

---

① It's the Dai custom to bury a newborn in a tree, implying that bad
things will never happen again in this family. Newborns are usually buried in
a different place from where their mothers are buried.

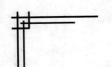

你要变成一只会唱的小鸟，
飞在一棵高高的树上，
在这里等着父亲。

"亲爱的桑洛呵！
我们的爱情，
像一棵竹子，
被劈成两半了。
连刚长出的竹笋，
也被人铲掉。

"桑洛呀！
快骑上马，
快来到森林吧！
我见不着你，
还有一只小鸟，
会代替我啼叫……"

娥并的声音渐渐低沉，
树林里显得更寂静。
树梢上出现一只小鸟，
不停地叫："桑洛！桑洛！"
猛根的三个姑娘，
扶着娥并，
听见小鸟的叫声，
心里更觉凄凉……

You will become a singing birdie,
fly up to a tall tree where you can,
and wait for your father."

"Oh, dear Sangluo!
Our love
is like a bamboo
split into two halves,
and even a fresh bamboo shoot
is grubbed up completely."

"Oh, Sangluo!
Please come to the forest on your horse!
If I can't see you anymore,
there will be a birdie
calling for you on behalf of me..."

E'bing's voice became weaker and lower,
and the forest was quieter and stiller.
Then a birdie appeared at a tree tip,
keeping tweeting: "Sangluo! Sangluo!"
The three young women of Menggen
holding up E'bing,
on hearing the birdie's sound,
felt even more heartbroken...

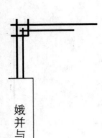

十二

桑洛还在撒网，
这天真不顺利，
没有网到一条鱼，
中午才回到家里。

走到门前楼梯下，
看见一缕缕的血迹，
桑洛问母亲：
"地上怎么会有血？
是哪家的孩子割破了手指？"

"儿呀！
今天我煮红树皮，
想给你的娥并染布，
染水倒在地上，
到处都染红了。"

12

Sangluo was still fishing,
but it was not his lucky day
that he caught nothing,
so he didn't get home until noon.

In front of the door and under the stairs,
he saw trails of blood
and asked his mother:
"Why is there blood to the ground?
Were any kid's fingers cut?"

"Oh, my son!
I was boiling some red bark①
to dye cloth for E'bing.
The water was poured onto the ground,
dyeing it red everywhere."

---

① Red bark is a local material for dyeing cloth or weavings in the Dai area.

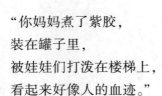

"你妈妈煮了紫胶，
装在罐子里，
被娃娃们打泼在楼梯上，
看起来好像人的血迹。"

母亲的话是在骗他，
桑洛心里一片惊疑，
他赶忙去问邻居，
邻近的人讲了实话：

"桑洛呀！
今天真是好日子，
喜事来到你家。
大象自己走到你家，
你家没有把它拴起来，
它又回到森林去了。

"一只羽毛闪亮的金孔雀，
已经飞上了你家的凉台。
可惜啊！
被你妈用箭射伤了，
金孔雀流着血飞走了……"

桑洛的心像着了火，
他跳上马就往寨外奔跑，

"Your mother also boiled some lac①
and put it in jars,
which were spilt by some kids on the stairs,
and looking like human blood."

Mother was lying,
and Sangluo was suspicious,
so he went in a hurry to ask his neighbors
who told him what really happened:

"Oh, Sangluo!
It was really a good day today,
for a happy event came to your home.
A big elephant came into your home by itself,
but though, your family didn't tie it to a post,
so it went back to the forest."

"A golden peacock with shiny feathers
flew onto your balcony.
Ah, it was such a pity!
It was shot with an arrow by your mother, injured,
and flew away, bleeding..."

Sangluo felt his heart in flames.
He jumped onto a horse, rushed out of the village

---

① Lac is a wax secretion of the lac insects after they take in the fluid
of trunks. It is used as the raw material in the Dai medicine.

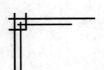

鞭子不停地把马抽打，
心里像有一盆火正在烧烤。

只见路上的血迹，
不见娥并的影子，
沙地上有一群小孩，
桑洛向他们打听：

"孩子们呀！
在热辣辣的太阳下，
这里有没有人走过？
是男是女快告诉我。"

"骑马的哥哥呀！
我们什么也没有看见，
只有三个姑娘，
扶着一个姑娘走过。

"四个姑娘都漂亮，
她们来时头上戴着鲜花，
她们去时哭声响遍树林。
最漂亮的姑娘周身流血，
像只受伤的金孔雀。"

"她们过去多久了？
能不能追得上？"
"只要你的马跑得快，
不久就能赶上。"

and kept whipping it from time to time.
He felt that a fire pan was burning in his chest.

He saw traces of blood on the road,
but there was no sight of E'bing.
Seeing some children playing in the sand,
he asked:

"Oh, children!
Under the scorching sun
were there any people passing?
Were they men or women? Please tell me."

"Oh, big brother on the horse!
We saw no one else
except three young women
helping one passing by."

"All of them were pretty,
wearing fresh flowers when they arrived,
but crying loudly when they went into the forest.
The prettiest one was bleeding all over,
like an injured golden peacock."

"How long has it been since they passed by?
Is it possible to catch up with them?"
"If your horse runs fast enough,
you can catch up with them soon."

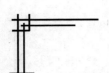

娥并与桑洛　E'bing and Sangluo

她们走过的河，
河水还是浑的，
河水还没有变清，
岸上还有她们的脚印。

桑洛催打着马，
又跑了一段路。
前面有个老大爹，
肩上扛着锄头。

"老伯呀，
你种田的时候，
看见有什么人走过？
请快告诉我。"

"不见，不见！
只有一朵鲜荷花，
去景多昂时开得正茂，
回来却被太阳晒焦，
花和叶子都变黄了。"

桑洛听了这些话，
心里更加难过。
他抽打着马，
使完了所有的力气，

The young women crossed the river
whose water was still unclear
with mud,
and the riverbank was still covered with their footprints.

Sangluo kept spurring the horse
to gallop for another while.
Then he saw an elderly man
with a hoe on his shoulder.

"Oh, uncle①!
When you farmed in the field today,
did you see some people passing by?
Please tell me."

"No, no!
I saw but a fresh lotus flower,
which bloomed at its prime on its way to Jingduo'ang,
but got burned on its return,
with both the flower and its leaves withering."

Sangluo, on hearing these words,
felt even sadder.
He kept whipping the horse
with all his strength

----

①　The uncle here doesn't mean a family member, but it's the Dai custom to call an elderly man politely who is not acquainted with.

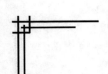

来到树林里。
一只小鸟在树上不停地叫：
"桑洛父亲，
桑洛父亲，
你来迟了！
你来迟了！"

小鸟是桑洛的血肉，
小鸟的叫声使桑洛伤心。
他在树下呆呆望着，
眼泪像夏天的雨水。

这是娥并生孩子的地方，
地上的树叶还是绿油油的；
小鸟在树上啼叫，
只是不见娥并。

"亲爱的姑娘！
等我一下吧！
再大的痛苦，
你也不要死去。

"你要等着你的桑洛，
我在马上像火烧，
痛苦无论多大，
你也要活着。"

and came into the forest.
A birdie cooing nonstop on a tree:
"Sangluo, father!
Sangluo, father!
You came too late!
You came too late!"

The birdie was Sangluo's flesh and blood,
whose cooing saddened Sangluo.
He stared blankly under the tree,
tears falling like the summer rain.

This was the place where E'bing gave birth to the child,
and the leaves on the ground were still green.
The birdie in the tree was still cooing,
but E'bing was nowhere to be seen.

"Dear young lady!
Please wait for me!
No matter how harrowing the pain,
don't die."

"Wait for your Sangluo,
and I am on my horse but feeling as if on a fire.
No matter how torturous my pain is,
stay alive."

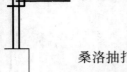

桑洛抽打着马，
眼泪不停地流，
来到猛根，
泪水已浸湿了鞍头。

跑进寨子什么也看不见，
只见娥并家门口挤满了人。
姑娘们正在舂米，
姑娘们正在劈柴。

桑洛下马就问：
"姑娘们为什么舂米？
姑娘们为什么劈柴？"

"我们舂米不是为了别的，
是为了桑洛的娥并；
我们劈柴不是拿去卖，
是为了你的娥并。
她前脚踏进门，
后脚还没进，
就倒下地死去了。"

Sangluo kept whipping the horse,
and his tears kept running down.
By the time he arrived at Menggen,
his tears had drenched the saddle.

Running into the village,
he saw but a crowd in front of E'bing's house.
Some young women were husking rice
and others were chopping firewood①.

Getting off the horse, Sangluo asked:
"Young ladies, why are you husking rice
and chopping firewood?"

"We husk rice for nothing else
but your E'bing;
we chop firewood not to sell
but for your E'bing.
As soon as she entered the door with one foot inside,
and the other one still outside,
she passed out."

---

①　On the day of one's death, the family members have only two meals
a day and husk the rice to cook for the relatives who come to help them out.

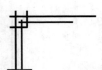

桑洛听见这些话，
天地都黑暗了。
他冲进娥并的屋子，
冲开挡路的人，
就像钻进了蜂房，
人们的哭声比打雷还响。

娥并的母亲坐在屋角流泪，
娥并静静地睡着，
还像活时一样美丽。

桑洛一下扑上去，
他抱起娥并，
痛苦地呼唤：

"醒醒吧！醒醒吧！
快伸开你的双手，
抱住你的桑洛；
快接住我的手帕，
擦去脸上的泪珠。

"我的好娥并！
你为什么紧紧闭着眼睛，
桑洛在和你说话，
你为什么不回答？

Sangluo, on hearing these words,
felt his whole world falling dark.
He rushed into E'bing's room,
elbowing his way.
He felt that he had got into a hive,
where the crying was louder than a thunder.

E'bing's mother was weeping at the corner of the room,
and E'bing seemed to be sleeping,
as pretty as if she were alive.

Sangluo jumped to bend down
and held her head up,
calling painfully:

"Wake up! Wake up!
Please stretch out your arms
to hold your Sangluo;
and use my handkerchief
to wipe off the tears on your face."

"My dear E'bing!
Why do you close your eyes so tightly,
for Sangluo is speaking to you right now,
but why don't you respond?"

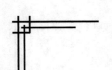

"你像天上栽的荷花，
芳香的荷花怎能凋谢？
你的哥哥啊！
没有修一个竹篷，
挡住夏天的雷雨。

"黑黑的头发，
黑黑的眉毛，
像棉花一样柔和的娥并啊！
即使你不能原谅我，
也要等一等我。

"像山一样的爱情，
被狂风吹倒；
留下桑洛一个人，
活着也不再有生命！

"如果你不能等待，
那就让我们的爱情，
像大青树的根子，
在深深的泥土里生存。"

娥并的眼睛，
微微张了三下，
看到了自己心爱的桑洛，
微笑着死在桑洛手上。

"You are like a lotus flower in the sky!
How could a fragrant lotus flower wither?
Ah, your big brother!
He didn't make you a bamboo tent
to shelter you from thunderstorms in the summer."

"With black hair
and black eyebrows,
oh, cotton-soft E'bing!
Even if you could not forgive me,
you should have waited for me."

"The love, as solid as a mountains,
has been destroyed by sterms;
now there is only Sangluo left,
and life will be lifeless!"

"If you can't wait,
then let our love
be like the root of a big green tree
living on deeply in soil."

E'bing opened her eyes
slightly for three times,
On seeing her beloved Sangluo,
she died, smiling, in his arms.

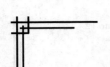

娥并与桑洛 E'bing and Sangluo

桑洛痛苦地呼唤，
双手紧紧把娥并拥抱：
"心爱的娥并啊，
你等等我吧！"
桑洛抽出了长刀！

大家慌忙拉他的手，
他抓出衣袋里的银子，
撒了满屋满地。
人们拥着去捡，
桑洛举起了刀……
倒在娥并身边。

Sangluo called out in agony,

with both arms holding her tightly:

"Ah, my beloved E'bing!

Do wait for me!"

Sangluo pulled out his long machete!

Everyone tried to stop him,

but he took out taels of silver from his pocket

and throw them all over the room.①

When people rushed to pick the silver,

he held up the machete...

and fell dead by her side.

---

①　In the Dai tradition, taels of silver are scattered in the house when one dies. Those who pick up the silver will be blessed for peace and safety.

十三

在一个长满青草的山坡，
有两个青年的坟墓，
人们叫作娥并山，
那里埋葬着娥并和桑洛。

为了让两个情人永难相见，
桑洛的母亲把坟墓也隔断，
放了三筒竹子隔开棺材，
用挑水的扁担挡在中间。

13

On a grass-capped hill,

there are two tombs for two youths.①

People call it E'bing mountain②,

where are buried E'bing and Sangluo.

To make sure that the two lovers would never see each other,

Sangluo's mother separated their tombs,

put three bamboo tubes between the two coffins,

and blocked the two further with a shoulder pole between

them.③

---

① According to the Dai's tradition, ordinary people are buried under
the ground after their death, but those with social status are cremated after
their death. Those who died of illness, murder or drowning are put into rivers, and bad luck is believed to go with the flowing water.

② Lovers are often buried together after their death in the place that
they used to hang out before.

③ It's Dai's local way to stop lovers from loving each other in another
world after their death.

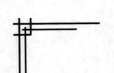

但是，爱情却隔不断，
好像娥并生前打水的井，
至今还没有枯干，
井水变得更甜。

水井旁有棵大青树，
树上还挂着娥并的腰带，
挑水的姑娘们，
常在树下怀念。

两个坟头上，
长起密密的芦苇。
芦苇的根连在一起，
芦苇的花絮在一起飞。

桑洛的母亲见了，
放一把火烧了芦苇，
火光中升起两颗星星，
这就是桑洛与娥并。

一颗星出现在黄昏，
一颗星出现在黎明。
年年三月两颗星相会在一起，
它们是那样明亮、美丽。

But, love is inseparable,

like the well, from which E'bing carried water when she was

alive,

has not dried even today,

and its water will be only sweeter.

By the well is a big green tree,

on which is E'bing's belt

and under which young women carring water

often commemorate her.

On the two tombs

reeds grow densely.

The reed roots are connected under the ground,

and the catkins keep flying together.

Seeing this,

Sangluo's mother set fire to the reeds,

but from the fire rose two stars:

they were Sangluo and E'bing.

One star appeared at twilight,

while the other one emerged at dawn.

In March① of every year, the two stars get together,

so brilliant and so beautiful.

---

① It is March in the Dai calendar.